Alfred W. (Alfred William) Pollard

Odes from the Greek Dramatists

Translated into Lyric Metres by English Poets and Scholars

Alfred W. (Alfred William) Pollard

Odes from the Greek Dramatists
Translated into Lyric Metres by English Poets and Scholars

ISBN/EAN: 9783744777544

Printed in Europe, USA, Canada, Australia, Japan

Cover: Foto ©Andreas Hilbeck / pixelio.de

More available books at **www.hansebooks.com**

TRANSLATED INTO LYRIC METRES
BY ENGLISH POETS AND SCHOLARS
EDITED BY ALFRED W. POLLARD

LONDON

DAVID STOTT, 370, OXFORD STREET, W.

MDCCCXC.

LONDON :

HENDERSON AND SPALDING, PRINTERS,

3 & 5, MARYLEBONE LANE, W.

TABLE OF CONTENTS.

PREFACE.

To the average school-boy the Chorus of a Greek Tragedy is an object of mingled hatred and derision—of derision, because at any call for action the attitude of the Chorus is generally characterized by helpless indecision—of hatred, because it was its wont to sing particularly hard Greek. Of the two feelings the hatred arising from the increased labour of "preparation" is probably the stronger, and in some cases it survives so long, that I have heard one of the most successful headmasters of modern times spitefully describe the great ode at the beginning of the *Agamemnon*, as "that chorus of Red Indians." Yet, all difficulties of text or interpretation notwithstanding, it may well be that the choral odes from which the Greek drama took its rise may prove in the end one of its most enduring claims to our admiration. The loss of the greater and, as we may conjecture, the better, part of the works of Pindar has raised these choral odes from the Greek dramatists to a position of greatly increased interest and importance, and there is a whole realm of Greek thought and of Greek religion to which they are our only guide. To print a collection of these odes apart from their contexts may at first sight seem a literary offence, but I would plead that the contexts are likely to be well known to most of my readers, and that in case this little volume should fall into any less learned hands I have in my "Notes" endeavoured briefly to indicate the relation of each chorus to the drama in which it occurs. To the objection that "nobody ever has translated a Greek chorus and nobody ever will," an answer is more difficult. Probably, those of my kind helpers who have approached most nearly to success would be the readiest to confess their failure ; but there are failures and failures, and where entire success, as in the great choruses of Æschylus, is manifestly impossible, to have failed splendidly establishes a claim to gratitude, which only ignorance or hyper-criticism will refuse to allow.

It will be observed that all the versions quoted in this volume have been made since the beginning of the present century. I have thus been able to avoid too violent diversities of style, while in my short Introduction and Bibliography I have endeavoured briefly to sketch the history of English verse translations of the Greek dramatists from the sixteenth century to our own time. I have only further to note, that after much consideration I have thought it better to adopt a uniform Greek text, that of the last Oxford edition of Dindorf's *Poetæ Scenici,* throughout my selection. Variations from this text in the editions used by translators I have endeavoured to record in my Notes.

The list of the obligations I have incurred in editing this little volume is a long one. I owe my best thanks to Prof. Campbell, Mr. A. E. Housman, Mr. Morshead, Mr. Ernest Myers, Mr. C. Kegan Paul, Mr. George Soutar, and Mr. A. W. Verrall for translations previously unpublished or specially made for this collection ; to

Prof. Campbell, Madame Darmesteter, Mr. Gladstone, Mr. Morshead, Miss Swanwick, Mr. Swinburne, Mr. Verrall, Judge Webb, Mr. Oscar Wilde, and Sir George Young for permission to quote translations already published; to the representatives of John Hookham Frere, Prof. Kennedy, and Thomas Love Peacock for similar courtesies; to Mr. John Murray for leave to use the translations of Dean Milman, and to Messrs. Bentley & Son, Kegan Paul, Trench & Co., Macmillan & Co., Pickering and Chatto, Ward and Lock, and the Cambridge Greek Play Committee for their cordial liberality. Mr. Browning's permission to use his translations from the *Hercules Furens* and that of Mrs. Browning from the *Prometheus Vinctus* I mention separately, because of the peculiarly kind letter (written from Venice only a few days before his last illness) by which it was accompanied. In closing the list of my obligations I wish also to acknowledge my great debt to Mr. F. W. Waldock for his unwearied pains in revising the Greek proofs, a task made unusually laborious both by the extreme delicacy of the type and the difficulty of ranging the English versions conveniently with their originals.

ALFRED W. POLLARD.

INTRODUCTION.

IN the Catalogue of the English Books published before 1640, of which copies exist in the British Museum, there is no entry of any kind under the heading Æschylus ; Sophocles is represented only by Watson's translation of the Antigone into Latin verse (*London*, 1581, 4to) ; Euripides, by three editions of the *Phœnissœ* as "translated and digested into Acte," under the name of *Jocasta*, by George Gascoigne and F. Kinwelmershe ; Aristophanes only by a Greek text of the *Knights*, published by J. Barnes at Oxford in 1593. The study of Greek made slow progress in England after the first enthusiasm begot by the Oxford Reformers had spent itself, but the dramatists fared even especially badly in comparison with other authors. Thus of Homer before 1640 there had appeared not only Chapman's renowned translation, of which successive instalments were issued between 1598 and 1616, but a Greek text printed by Bishop in 1591, a *Clavis Homerica*, and versions of the *Batrachomyomachia* by Fowldes, and of ten books of the Iliad translated by Hall from the French. Of Herodotus, as Mr. Lang has lately reminded us, Barnaby Rich Englished the first and second books in 1584. Thucydides had been translated through the French as early as 1550, and the version by the philosopher Hobbes appeared in 1629. The *Cyro-*

pædia and the *Œconomicus* of Xenophon also existed in numerous forms, and the *Anabasis* found a translator in J. Bingham in 1623. The list could easily be extended, but is perhaps already long enough to prove our point that in the 16th Century the dramatists were among the least favoured of the Greek classics. With professed scholars, amid whom we must reckon some learned and royal ladies, they certainly found a home. In his *Apologie for Poetrie* Sir Philip Sidney quotes from the *Ajax* and the *Medea*, and we know that the works of Sophocles and Euripides formed part of the library of Mary, Queen of Scots. In Ascham's *Scolemaster* these two authors are frequently referred to. In his judgment—

> " In Tragedies (the goodliest Argument of All, and for the use, either of a learned preacher or a civill gentleman, more profitable than Homer, Pindar, Virgill and Horace, yea, comparable in myne opinion, with the doctrine of Aristotle, Plato, and Xenophon), the Grecians, Sophocles and Euripides, far over-match our Seneca in Latin, namely in οἰκονομίᾳ *et decoro*, although Senecaes elocution and verse be verie commendable for his tyme."

In another place Ascham reckons all the four Greek dramatists of whom we possess works as among the authors "of which, I thank God, even my poor studie lacketh not one." We may conjecture, however, without serious injustice, that he was somewhat less familiar with Æschylus than with Sophocles and Euripides, whom he quotes and praises much more freely. The unfortunate lacuna by which in the *editio princeps* of Æschylus (Venice, 1518) no less than 1268 verses were omitted from the *Agamemnon*, must have seriously damaged the poet's fame, and even if Ascham possessed the 1552 edition, the first in which the mistake was rectified, the labours of some generations of commentators were needed before the splendour of the greatest Greek poet could be fully appreciated.   It may be mentioned that one play of Aristophanes, and perhaps only one, the *Plutus*, in which he turns his back on the Old Comedy, was certainly popular in the 16th century.   John Dorne, the Oxford bookseller, sold nearly a dozen copies of it, mostly however in Latin, in the course of a single year.   Of the other plays we hear little or nothing till the edition of the *Equites* by Barnes in 1593.

The *Jocasta* of Gascoigne and Kinwelmershe has some claim on our attention, not only as the first English imitation of a Greek tragedy, but also for its intrinsic merits, which are not inconsiderable.   The play was composed in 1566, and of its five acts Gascoigne was responsible for the second, third, and last, and his collaborator for the first and fourth.   Their treatment of their original was exceedingly free, and in the choruses they borrow little more than a general idea.   Chaucer's seven-line stanza was their favourite metre, and in the following variation on the theme ὦ πολύμοχθος Ἄρης (*Phœnissæ*, 783, etc.), Gascoigne uses it with fine effect.

> O fierce and furious God, whose harmfull harte,
> Rejoyceth most to shed the giltlesse blood,
> Whose headie wil doth all the world subvert,
> And doth envie the pleasant mery moode,
> Of our estate that erst in quiet stoode,
> Why doest thou thus our harmeless towne annoye
> Which mightie Bacchus governed in joye?

Father of warre and death, that dost remove
With wrathfull wrecke from wofull mothers' breast,
The trustie pledges of their tender love,
So graunt the Gods, that for our finall rest,
Dame Venus' pleasant lookes may please thee best,
Wherby when thou shalt all amazed stand,
The sword may fall out of thy trembling hand.

And thou maist prove some other way full well
The bloudie prowesse of thy mightie speare,
Wherwith thou raisest from the depth of hell,
The wrathfull sprites of all the furies there,
Who when they wake, do wander every where,
And never rest to range aboute the coastes,
T' enriche that pit with spoile of damned ghostes.

And when thou hast our fieldes forsaken thus,
Let cruell discorde beare thee companie,
Engirt with snakes and serpents venemous,
Even she that can with red vermilion dye
The gladsome greene that florished pleasantly,
And make the greedie grounde a drinking cup,
To sup the bloud of murdered bodyes up.

Yet thou returne, O joye and pleasant peace,
From whence thou didst against our will departe,
Ne let thy worthie minde from travell cease,
To chase disdaine out of the poysoned harte,
That raised warre to all our paynes and smarte,
Even from the brest of Œdipus his sonne,
Whose swelling pride hath all this jarre begonne.

And thou, great God, that doth all things decree,
And sitst on highe above the starrie skies,
Thou chiefest cause of causes all that bee,
Regard not his offence but heare our cries,
And speedily redresse our miseries ;
For what can we poore wofull wretches doe
But crave thy aide, and onely cleave thereto ?

There is some good poetry in this, especially in the fourth stanza, but very little of Euripides. Yet, had the drama in England followed the course which Sir Philip Sidney unwisely desired for it, Gascoigne's *Jocasta* might well claim to be reckoned as a landmark in its history. Happily, however, for England, the hot blood that ran in the veins of the Elizabethan poets refused to be regulated by the frigidity of Seneca, or even by the more human example of Euripides, and the *Jocasta* remained without an imitator. Putting aside minute points, such as possible reminiscences of Aristophanes in Ben Jonson, it may be said broadly that the English drama, in the age when it attained its most splendid development, was not only uninfluenced by, but superbly unconscious of, its Greek predecessor. Lovers of English literature have, on the whole, no cause to regret this unconsciousness ; nor, in any case, is this the place to consider how far it might have been possible for classical models to have steadied without deadening the tumultuous life which in our English dramatists, so quickly wore itself to decay.

One thing only, from the special point of view of this volume, we may surely regret—that no one of the greater Elizabethans ever deigned to translate a lyric passage from his Attic forerunners. The translation would very possibly have been inaccurate ; so are Shelley's. But, as with Shelley, so with the Elizabethan lyrists, in even the second-best of their verse there is a magic and a charm which we look for in vain in numberless poe's not undeservedly called great, and which is rarely found in translations, even at their best. For a play of Æschylus translated by Marlowe, for a play of Sophocles translated by Shakespeare, for a play of Euripides translated by Webster, it is idle to speculate what we could afford to surrender in exchange; but we may well hurl our curse at the slothfulness of the English scholars who left Shakespeare to search for his classical themes in North's Plutarch, and would not provide the greatest of all adapters with a prose version of a Greek dramatist from which to steal.

The century which followed the composition of *Jocasta* thus contains few facts of any importance for the history of the Greek drama in England. In 1649 such similarity as could be traced between the execution of Charles I. and the murder of Agamemnon induced Christopher Wase to publish at the Hague a very poor verse translation of the *Electra*, which he dedicated to the Princess Elizabeth. In 1651 appeared T. Randolph's prose comedy, *Hey for Honesty! Down with Knavery!* founded on the *Plutus* of Aristophanes, and eight years later a more formal translation was made by a certain H. B. Besides these works, we need only note, in passing, the affection of Milton for Euripides, his hesitation between tragic and epic models for his *Paradise Lost*, and his adoption of the form of Greek tragedy for his *Samson Agonistes* (1671). But in 1663 Thomas Stanley published, in London, his notable edition of Æschylus, with a Latin translation and commentary; and two years later there appeared, at Cambridge, the first instalment of a Greek and Latin edition of Sophocles. Of Euripides, whose popularity in England had begun so much earlier than that of Æschylus, a complete edition was delayed until 1694 (*J. Hayes: Cantabrigiæ*), and the Aristophanes published in 1695 only contained two plays, the *Plutus* and the *Clouds*. But we may reckon that by the end of the seventeenth century the study of the Greek dramatist had engaged the serious attention of English scholars, and begin to look for its results in more popular forms.

As we have seen, the *Jocasta* of Gascoigne bore only a distant resemblance to the *Phœnissœ*, its nominal original and Wase's *Electra* is beneath contempt. The first important verse translations from the Greek tragedians must thus be assigned to the beginning of the eighteenth century. The honour of publishing them belongs to Bernard Lintott, who appears to have planned an elaborate series of monthly volumes, the progress of which was prematurely stopped, probably from want of sufficient support. The first volume of the series was an anonymous version (by Lewis Theobald) of the *Ajax* of Sophocles; and in justice to Lintott's memory I quote some sentences of His address, "The Publisher to the Reader," as a record of his good intentions :—

> " The Reputation of the Ancient Greek Tragedy is so univer-
> sally known, that there can be no occasion for an apology to
> usher in a Translation of 'em. I will only beg leave, therefore,
> to acquaint you with my present Design in the prosecution of
> that Attempt and the manner in which I intend to execute it.
> " I have by me the Tragedies of Æschylus, Sophocles, and
> Euripides, Translated into English blank Verse; they are all,
> as I have been assur'd by several Gentlemen of allow'd Judg-
> ment in these Matters, very exactly done from the Greek; the
> sense of the several Authors is everywhere very faithfully given;
> and where-ever the regard which was necessary to be had to our
> own Language would allow of it, the Translation is so near the

Original, as to be of use to the Learners of the Greek Language, by the assistance it may give them in the construction of these Authors ; and wherever the Translators have been obliged to take more than ordinary Liberty in departing from the words of the Text, Care is taken at the same time to give the literal interpretation of the Greek in the Notes. Tho' this Translation (as it is but a Translation, and by its nature consequently confin'd and cramp'd in the Diction) may not come up to that Beauty of Language and Expression which is to be found in some of the best of our Original English Tragedies; yet it is hop'd that nothing will be found in the Stile, that is either Cold, Mean, or absolutely below this kind of Writing . . .

"I have given the publick the Ajax of Sophocles as a specimen of my Undertaking. If they think fit to encourage it, I intend to give 'em one every Month, till I have gone thro' all the Greek Tragedies.

"I had forgot to observe, that when the Works of any one Author (as Æschylus) are compleated, there will be an Account of his Life, and a proper Critical Preface prefix'd before 'em."

The anonymous version of the *Ajax* (1714), to which Lintott prefixed this modest address, was followed by the *Electra* (1714) and the *Œdipus Tyrannus* (1715), to both of which Theobald put his name, dedicating the former to Addison and the latter to the Earl of Rockingham. Who were the other members of Lintott's band of translators we have no means of knowing, for the series never went beyond the third volume. It is possible that Theobald contemplated executing the whole series himself, as in 1715, when Lintott was presumably tired of the speculation, prose versions of the *Clouds* and the *Plutus* of Aristophanes were published for Theobald by Jonas Brown. The following chorus from the *Œdipus Rex* shows the translator at his best, and I therefore give it as a specimen of his powers :—

O may it ever be my Fate
Justly those sacred Truths to rate;
And those blest Laws that have their Rise
From Wisdom lodg'd above the Skies,
Those which the Olympian King alone
Dictates from his eternal Throne,
(Unlike to those weak mortals frame),
Live unabolish'd, still the same!
Sprung from the God, replete with heav'nly Fire,
They baffle Time, and keep their Strength entire.

The Tyrant and illegal Man
From Pride and rash Contempt began;
Pride and Contempt that left him high
O'er Mountains of Impiety;
Till plac'd aloft he dazzled grows,
And in his Fear his Hold foregoes.
O! may the City's Cares succeed,
Nor envying Fates their search mislead.
With ardent humble Prayr's the Gods I'll move;
The Gods shall still my kind Protectors prove!

But whoe'er in Word or Deed
Does from the sacred Laws recede,
No divine Resentments fearing,
Nor the hallow'd Shrines revering,
If licentious Ease beguile him,
If dishonest Gains defile him,
If he pursue corrupting Pleasure,
Or grasps at unpermitted Treasure,
Some rigid Doom his Guilt o'ertake!
Else who hereafter will controul
The Sallies of his impious Soul?
If no avenging Judgments shake
The triumphs of the dissolute,
'Tis time th' instructive Choirs be mute.

Let mistaking zeal no more
The Truths of Oracles adore;
No more to th' Lycian Temples pressing,
Or th' Olympian God addressing

If Apollo do not right him
On the impious doubts, that slight him :
But thou Eternal Jove ! that bearest
Rule Universal ; if thou hearest
The dire Neglect, avenge thy Son.
For all th' Oracl'ous Truths of old,
That were to wretched Laius told,
Have lost their credit and Renown.
Apollo's Honours sink apace,
All the Deity gives place.

Though Lintott's projected series came to an untimely
end, the study of the Greek dramatists continued to
make its way during the first half of the eighteenth
century. It may rather, however, be said to have shared
in the increased attention devoted to Greek poetry in
general, as witnessed by the success of Pope's Homer
and by the versions of *Sappho* and *Anacreon* by Ambrose
Philipps, than to have itself specially advanced in public
favour. The *Hecuba* of Euripides formed the ground-
work of a tragedy published by Richard West in 1726,
and another version was made by T. Morell in 1749, a
year which also saw the publication of a rendering of the
Iphigeneia in Tauris as part of Gilbert West's edition of
Pindar. In 1758 a renewed attempt was made to
present the complete works of a Greek dramatist in an
adequate English translation, and this time with better
success. The translator was Thomas Francklin, Professor
of Greek in the University of Cambridge ; and the two
handsome quarto volumes of his version of Sophocles
were dedicated, by special permission, to the Prince of
Wales, and subscribed for by so many noblemen, states-
men, and classical scholars, that their names fill twenty

columns. Francklin has lately been acclaimed as the best of the eighteenth century translators from the dramatists—no very high distinction—and he is perhaps a little less purely declamatory than Potter; but the following version of a chorus from the *Trachiniæ* does not impress me as the work of a great artist, though I think it is at least a fair specimen of the translator's powers :—

On thee we call, great god of day
To whom the night, with all her starry train,
   Yields her solitary reign,
To send us some propitious ray :
Say thou, whose all-beholding eye
   Doth nature's every part descry,
What dang'rous ocean, or what land unknown
From Deianira keeps Alcmena's valiant son.

For she nor joy nor comfort knows,
But weeps her absent lord, and vainly tries
To close her ever-streaming eyes,
   Or sooth her sorrows to repose :
Like the sad bird of night, alone
She makes her solitary moan ;
And still, as on her widow'd bed reclin'd
She lyes, unnumber'd fears perplex her anxious mind.

Ev'n as the troubled billows roar,
When angry Boreas rules th' inclement skies
And waves on waves tumultuous rise
   To lash the Cretan shore :
Thus sorrows still on sorrows prest,
   Fill the great Alcides' breast ;
Unfading yet shall his fair virtues bloom,
And some protecting god preserve him from the tomb.

Wherefore, to better thoughts inclin'd,
Let us with hope's fair prospect fill thy breast,
Calm thy anxious thoughts to rest,
    And ease thy troubled mind :
No bliss on man, unmix'd with woe,
Doth Jove, great lord of all, bestow ;
But good with ill and pleasure still with pain,
Like heaven's revolving signs, alternate reign.

Not always do the shades of night remain,
    Nor ever with hard fate is man oppress'd ;
The wealth that leaves us may return again,
    Sorrow and joy successive fill the breast.
        Fearless then of every ill,
        Let cheerful hope support thee still ;
Remember, queen, there is a pow'r above ;
And when did the great Father, careful Jove,
Forget his children dear, and kind paternal love?

Francklin's translation appears to have been regarded as a success ; and a new edition was published in 1766, with the addition of a dissertation on Greek tragedy by the translator. In the year of its first publication (1759) interest in the Greek theatre had also been fanned by an English version of Père Brumoy's *Théâtre des Grecs*, in which Mrs. Lennox was assisted by several English scholars, amongst others, by Dr. Johnson. In 1774, Michael Wodhull (now, perhaps, best known as a collector of books and an employer of the most famous of English binders, Roger Payne) issued proposals for a translation of Euripides. but his leisurely methods of work caused him to be anticipated by Robert Potter, Vicar of Lowestoft, among whose defects that of lack of industry can assuredly not be reckoned. To Potter belongs the unique distinction of having rendered into

English verse the whole of the tragedies of Æschylus, Sophocles, and Euripides, which have come down to us intact. His version of Æschylus appeared in 1777-78, and reached a second edition the following year. In 1781 he published the first volume of his Euripides, and the second in 1783. But here he had no longer the field to himself, for in 1780 had appeared an anonymous translation (by J. Bannister) of four tragedies of Euripides, and in 1782 Wodhull, awakened from his sleep, produced, in four quarto volumes, a version, not only of the nineteen tragedies still extant, but of the Fragments as well. Under these circumstances, it is hardly surprising that none of the rival translations attained, during the century in which it was issued, the honours of a second edition. Potter's friends, however, urged him to continue his task; and, undaunted by the comparative failure of his Euripides, or by the high reputation of the existing version by Francklin, he set to work on the tragedies of Sophocles; and in 1788 this last fruit of his classical labours was issued from the press.

Of Potter's merits as a translator, more particularly as a translator of choral odes, it is not easy to speak quite fairly. Some tenderness is due to a man of so much industry and enthusiasm, and, when viewed in connection with the poetry of the time, his work will appear something more than creditable. When Dr. Johnson published his depreciatory estimate of Gray, Potter became the poet's apologist; and his choral translations are not without traces of Gray's influence. Here is a bit from the *Septem contra Thebas*, which seems to me a fair example of his work:

Woe, woe, intolerable woe !
Fierce from their camps the hosts advance,
Before their march with thund'ring tread
Proud o'er the plain their fiery coursers prance,
And hither bend their footsteps dread :
Yon cloud of dust that chokes the air,
A true tho' tongueless messenger,
Marks plain the progress of the foe.
And now the horrid clash of arms,
That, like the torrent, whose impetuous tide
Roars down the mountain's craggy side,
Shook the wide fields with fierce alarms,
With nearer terrors strikes our souls,
And thro' our chaste recesses rolls :
Hear, all ye pow'rs of Heav'n, propitious hear,
And check the furies of this threat'ning war !

This is fair declamatory verse ; and, both in his choruses
and his decasyllabics (as, for instance, in the speech of
Hæmon to Creon in the *Antigone*) it is in declamation
that Potter shows to the best advantage. But, though in
his comparative lyrical incapacity he belongs to the poets
of an older school, his work has some claims to attention
in relation to the great outburst of poetry which marked
the opening years of the nineteenth century. It is surely
noteworthy that the decade which heralded the poetical
return to Nature in the first works of Burns, Cowper,
and Crabbe, was the same in which the complete works
of the Greek tragedians were for the first time made
accessible to English readers. There is the less reason
to suppose the coincidence to have been purely acci-
dental when we look forward to the years in which
Wordsworth, Scott, Byron, and Coleridge were writing
their best. Potter died in 1804, at a great age, having
seen only one of his translations attain a second edition.

But in 1808 all his three versions were reprinted, and new editions of his Æschylus were published in 1809 and 1819, and of his Euripides in 1814. In 1809 also re-issues were demanded, both of Francklin's Sophocles and of Wodhull's Euripides. The poets of the beginning of the century were too busy with great original work to give themselves seriously to the labour of translation ; and Potter, Wodhull, and Francklin were allowed to retain the field. But, under the influence of Porson, English scholarship had at last fully awakened to the splendour of the Greek drama, and the number of texts and critical editions published between 1800 and 1830 affords the greatest possible contrast to our previous apathy.

The revival of the practice of translation began with Mitchell's Aristophanes (1820-22). Boyd's version of the *Agamemnon* followed in 1823 ; and three other translations of this play were published before the close of 1832 —the most noticeable that by John Symmons, the others by J. S. Harford and Thomas Medwin, the friend of Shelley. In 1824 a new version of Sophocles was published by the Rev. Thomas Dale, of Corpus Christi College, Cambridge. This has never been reprinted, but has certainly more poetic merit than either Francklin's or Potter's. The following chorus from the *Œdipus Coloneus* is far too free a paraphrase to deserve enthusiastic praise, but in rhythm and feeling affords an agreeable change to the turgid rhetoric of earlier versions :—

If to thee, eternal Queen,
Empress of the worlds unseen ;
Mighty Pluto, if to thee,
Hell's terrific Deity,
Lips of mortal mould may dare
Breathe the solemn suppliant prayer,
Grant the stranger swift release,
Bid the mourner part in peace,
Guide him where in silence deep
All that once were mortal sleep.
Since relentless Fate hath shed
Sorrows o'er thy guiltless head,
In thy pangs let mercy stay thee,
In the grave let rest repay thee.

Powers of Night ! Infernal Maids !
Monster-guardian of the shades !
Who, as antique legends tell,
Keep'st the brazen porch of Hell,
And with ceaseless yell dost rave
Fearful from thy gloomy cave ;
Thou, whose mighty bulk of yore
Earth to sable Tartarus bore ;
Veil thy terrors, quell thine anger,
Gently meet the passing stranger,
Sinking now with welcome speed
To the dwellings of the dead.
Thou, the ward of Hell who keepest !
Thou, the guard who never sleepest !

The merits and defects of this translation are closely
similar to those which mark the work of Joseph Anstice,
one of the earliest translators, whom I have laid under
contribution for the present volume. Anstice's versions
are almost always full of music and grace, though they
lack power, and too frequently descend to mere paraphrase. The publication of his volume of choruses, save

in its single authorship and the absence of the Greek text, so closely similar in plan to my own, may fully bring to a close this brief survey of the most noteworthy translations from the Greek dramatists, down to the period from which my selection begins.

ALFRED W. POLLARD.

ÆSCHYLUS.

PROMETHEUS VINCTUS.

398—434.

στένω σε τᾶς οὐλυμένας   στρ.
τύχας, Προμηθεῦ,
†ακρυσίστακτον δ᾽ ἀπ᾽ ὄσσων
ῥαδινῶν λειβομένα ῥέος παρειὰν
νοτίοις ἔτεγξα παγαῖς·
ἀμέγαρτα γὰρ τάδε Ζεὺς
ἰδίοις νόμοις κρατύνων
ὑπερήφανον θεοῖς τοῖς
†πάρος ἐν, δείκνυσιν αἰχμάν.   *P...*

πρόπασα δ᾽ ἤδη στονόεν   ἀντ.
λέλακε χώρα,
μεγαλοσχήμονα τ᾽ ἀρχαι-
οπρεπῆ * * στένουσι τὰν σὰν
ξυνομαιμόνων τε τιμὰν,
ὁπόσοι τ᾽ ἔποικον ἁγνᾶς
Ἀσίας ἕδος νέμονται,
μεγαλοστόνοισι σοῖς πή-
μασι συγκάμνουσι θνητοί·

Κολχίδος τε γᾶς ἔνοικοι   στρ.
παρθένοι, μάχας ἄτρεστοι,
καὶ Σκύθης ὅμιλος, οἳ γᾶς
ἔσχατον τόπον ἀμφὶ Μαιῶ-
τιν ἔχουσι λίμναν,

Ἀραβίας τ᾽ ἄρειον ἄνθος,   ἀντ.
ὑψίκρημνόν θ᾽ οἳ πόλισμα
Καυκάσου πέλας νέμονται,
δάϊος στρατὸς, ὀξυπρῴροι-
σι βρέμων ἐν αἰχμαῖς.

PROMETHEUS VINCTUS.

398—434.

I MOAN thy fate, I moan for thee,
   Prometheus! From my eyes too tender,
Drop after drop incessantly
   The tears of my heart's pity render
My cheeks wet from their fountains free;
   Because that Zeus, the stern and cold,
     Whose law is taken from his breast,
     Uplifts his sceptre manifest
      Over the gods of old.

All the land is moaning
With a murmured plaint to-day;
   All the mortal nations
   Having habitations
In the holy Asia
   Are a dirge entoning
For thine honour and thy brothers',
Once majestic beyond others
   In the old belief,—
Now are groaning in the groaning
   Of thy deep-voiced grief.

Mourn the maids inhabitant
   Of the Colchian land,
Who with white, calm bosoms stand
   In the battle's roar:
Mourn the Scythian tribes that haunt
The verge of earth, Mæotis' shore.

Yea! Arabia's battle-crown
And dwellers in the beetling town
Mount Caucasus sublimely nears,—
An iron squadron, thundering down
   With the sharp-prowed spears.

μόνον δὴ πρόσθεν ἄλλον ἐν πόνοις
ἐαμίντ ἀκαμαντοδέτοις
Τιτᾶνα λύμαις εἰσιδόμαν θεὸν
Ἄτλαν, ὃς αἰὲν ὑπέροχον σθένος
κραταιὸν γᾶς οὐράνιόν τε πόλον
νώτοις ὀχῶν στενάζει.
βοᾷ δὲ πόντιος κλύδων
ξυμπίτνων, στένει βυθός,
κελαινὸς Ἄϊδος δ᾽ ὑποβρέμει μυχὸς γᾶς,
παγαί θ᾽ ἁγνορύτων ποταμῶν
στένουσιν ἄλγος οἰκτρόν.

PROMETHEUS VINCTUS.

887—906.

ἦ σοφὸς ἦ σοφὸς ὃς   στρ.
πρῶτος ἐν γνώμᾳ τόδ᾽ ἐβάστασε καὶ γλώσ-
σᾳ διεμυθολόγησεν,
ὡς τὸ κηδεῦσαι καθ᾽ ἑαυ-
τὸν ἀριστεύει μακρῷ·
καὶ μήτε τῶν πλού-
τῳ διαθρυπτομένων
μήτε τῶν γέννᾳ μεγαλυνομένων
ὄντα χερνήταν ἐραστεῦσαι γάμων.

But one other before have I seen to remain
   By invincible pain
Bound and vanquished,—one Titan ! 'twas Atlas, who
  bears
In a curse from the gods, by that strength of his own
   Which he evermore wears,
The weight of the heaven on his shoulder alone,
   While he sighs up the stars ;
And the tides of the ocean wail bursting their bars,—
   Murmurs still the profound,
And black Hades roars up through the chasm of the
  ground,
And the fountains of pure-running rivers moan low
   In a pathos of woe.

     ELIZABETH BARRETT BROWNING.

PROMETHEUS VINCTUS.

887—906.

OH, wise was he, oh, wise was he
Who first within his spirit knew,
And with his tongue declared it true,
That love comes best that comes unto
   The equal of degree !
And that the poor and that the low
Should seek no love from those above
Whose souls are fluttered with the flow
Of airs about their golden height,
Or proud because they see a-row
   Ancestral crowns of light.

μήποτε μήποτέ μ᾽, ὦ
πότνιαι Μοῖραι λεχέων Διὸς εὐνά-
τειραν ἴδοισθε πέλουσαν· ε ι ς ...
μηδὲ πλαθείην γαμέτᾳ
τινὶ τῶν ἐξ οὐρανοῦ.
ταρβῶ γὰρ ἀστερ-
γάνορα παρθενίαν
εἰσορῶσ᾽ Ἰοῦς μέγα δαπτομέναν
δυσπλάνοις Ἥρας ἀλατείαις πόνων.

ἐμοὶ δ᾽ ὅτι μὲν ὁμαλὸς ὁ γάμος
ἄφοβος, οὐ δέδια, μηδὲ κρεισ-
σόνων θεῶν ἔρως ἄφυ- . . . .
κτον ὄμμα προσδράκοι με.
ἀπόλεμος ὅδε γ᾽ ὁ πόλεμος, ἄπορα
πόριμος· οὐδ᾽ ἔχω τίς ἂν γενοίμαν.
τὰν Διὸς γὰρ οὐχ ὁρῶ
μῆτιν ὅπα φύγοιμ᾽ ἄν.

Oh, never, never may ye, Fates,
  Behold me with your awful eyes,
  Lift mine too fondly up the skies
Where Zeus upon the purple waits !
  Nor let me step too near—too near
To any suitor, bright from heaven :
  Because I see, because I fear
This loveless maiden vexed and laden
By this fell curse of Herè, driven
  On wanderings dread and drear.

Nay, grant an equal troth instead
  Of nuptial love, to bind me by !
It will not hurt, I shall not dread
  To meet it in reply.
But let not love from those above
Revert and fix me, as I said,
  With that inevitable Eye !
I have no sword to fight that fight,
I have no strength to tread that path,
I know not if my nature hath
The power to bear, I cannot see
Whither from Zeus's infinite
I have the power to flee.

ELIZABETH BARRETT BROWNING.

SEPTEM CONTRA THEBAS.

720—791.

πέφρικα τὰν ὠλεσίοικον   στρ. α΄.
θεὸν, οὐ θεοῖς ὁμοίαν,
παναληθῆ, κακόμαντιν
πατρὸς εὐκταίαν Ἐρινὺν
τελέσαι τὰς περιθύμους
κατάρας Οἰδιπόδα βλαψίφρονος.
παιδολέτωρ᾽ δ᾽ ἔρις ἅδ᾽ ὀτρύνει.

ξένος δὲ κλήρους ἐπινωμᾷ   ἀντ. α΄.
Χάλυβος Σκυθῶν ἄποικος,
κτεάνων χρηματοδαίτας
πικρὸς, ὠμόφρων σίδαρος,
χθόνα ναίειν διαπήλας,
ὁπόσαν καὶ φθιμένοισιν κατέχειν,
τῶν μεγάλων πεδίων ἀμοίρους.

ἐπειδὰν αὐτοκτόνως   στρ. β΄.
αὐτοδάϊκτοι θάνωσι,
καὶ χθονία κόνις πίῃ
μελαμπαγὲς αἷμα φοίνιον,
τίς ἂν καθαρμοὺς πόροι,
τίς ἂν σφε λούσειεν; ὦ
πόνοι δόμων νέοι παλαι-
οῖσι συμμιγεῖς κακοῖς.

SEPTEM CONTRA THEBAS.

720—791.

I AM shuddering with sad fear
Of the ruin hovering near,—
Lest the power of godless might
Alien from the lords of light,
Seer infallible of ill,
Dark Erinnys, should fulfil
Œdipus' infatuate vows
'Gainst the children of his house.
Still she holds her destined path,
Prompted by a father's wrath.
Now this child-destroying strife
Lends her purpose instant life.

Ruthless Iron sways the lot
That shall portion them the plot
Each shall hold.   A stranger he
From the Scythian colony
Once that passed the Pontic deep
To Chalybia's country steep.
Stern divider, judge severe!
What possession find they here?
What their heritage?   So much
As the dead man's corpse may touch,
So much either shall obtain;
Nothing more of all yon plain.

When fratricidal death
Hath stopped their raging breath,
And Earth's dust drunk deep draughts of sinful gore,
What charm may purge the guilt
Of blood so foully spilt?
Whose hand shall bathe them?—O unhappy store
Of fresh woes for this house, blent with the woes before!

παλαιγενῆ γὰρ λέγω   ἀντ. β'.
παρβασίαν ὠκύποινον·
αἰῶνα δ' ἐς τρίτον μένει·
Ἀπόλλωνος εὖτε Λάϊος
βίᾳ, τρὶς εἰπόντος ἐν
μεσομφάλοις Πυθικοῖς
χρηστηρίοις θνᾴσκοντα γέν-
νας ἄτερ σώζειν πόλιν.

κρατηθεὶς δ' ἐκ φίλων ἀβουλίαις   στρ. γ'.
ἐγείνατο μὲν μόρον αὑτῷ,
πατροκτόνον Οἰδιπόδαν,
ὅστε μὴ πρὸς ἁγνὰν
σπείρας ἄρουραν, ἵν' ἐτράφη,
ῥίζαν αἱματόεσσαν
ἔτλα. παράνοια συνᾶγε
νυμφίους φρενώλεις·

κακῶν δ' ὥσπερ θάλασσα κῦμ' ἄγει·   ἀντ. γ'.
τὸ μὲν πίτνον, ἄλλο δ' ἀείρει
τρίχαλον, ὃ καὶ περὶ πρύ-
μναν πόλεως καχλάζει.
μεταξὺ δ' ἀλκὰ δι' ὀλίγου
τείνει πύργος ἐν εὔρει.
δέδοικα δὲ σὺν βασιλεῦσι
μὴ πόλις δαμασθῇ.

τέλειαι γὰρ παλαιφάτων ἀρᾶν   στρ. δ'.
βαρεῖαι καταλλαγαί,
τὰ δ' ὀλοὰ πελόμεν' οὐ παρέρχεται.
πρύπρυμνα δ' ἐκβολὰν φέρει
ἀνδρῶν ἀλφηστᾶν
ὄλβος ἄγαν παχυνθείς.

I mean that ancient crime
Rued by all after-time—
Three generations now have borne the weight—
Since, braving Phœbus' word,
Thrice from the tripod heard,
How 'twas the constant will of sovran Fate,
That dying without seed he should preserve the state,

Laius by love o'ercome
Begat his own sure doom,
Sad Œdipus, the slayer of his sire,
Who ploughed the fields where erst
His infant bones were nurst,
And sowed a crop that bloomed in murderous ire.
Infatuate bride and groom, so drawn by mad desire !

Evils are like a surge,
Where billows billows urge ;—
Each peers three-crested o'er the wave that's gone,
Thundering abaft the helm
And threatening to o'erwhelm
The frail defence that braves that waste alone.
I fear lest with her kings Thebes may be now o'erthrown.

When dawns the fate-appointed Day,
The aged curse is hard to allay.
Once here, Destruction rides not past,
Till those are fallen beneath the blast,
Whose toil-earned wealth, too highly heaped,
Brings ruin ;—and the man hath reaped
But sacrifice of all at last.

τίν' ἀνδρῶν γὰρ τοσόνδ' ἐθαύμασαν   ἀντ. δ'.
θεοὶ καὶ ξυνέστιοι
πόλεος ὁ πολύβοτός τ' αἰὼν βροτῶν,   . ͵
ὗσαν τότ' Οἰδίπουν τίον,   ·͵
τὰν ἁρπαξάνδραν
κῆρ' ἀφελόντα χώρας;

ἐπεὶ δ' ἀρτίφρων   στρ. ε'.
ἐγένετο μέλεος ἀθλίων
γάμων, ἐπ' ἄλγει δυσφορῶν
μαινομένᾳ κραδίᾳ
δίδυμα κάκ' ἐτέλεσεν·
πατροφόνῳ χερὶ τῶν
κρεισσοτέκνων ὀμμάτων ἐπλάγχθη.

τέκνοισιν δ' ἀρὰς   ἀντ. ε'.
ἐφῆκεν ἐπικότους τροφᾶς,
αἰαῖ, πικρογλώσσους ἀρὰς,
καὶ σφε σιδαρονόμῳ
διὰ χερὶ ποτὲ λαχεῖν
κτήματα· νῦν δὲ τρέω
μὴ τελέσῃ καμψίπους Ἐρινύς.

Who more admired of gods and men
Than Œdipus was honoured then
By all who shared the city's hearth,
Drawing rich life from Theban earth,
When he had freed the land from fear
Of the Sphinx monster seated near,
Dire minister of death and dearth?

But when he came to know
The measure of his woe,
That wretched wedlock with dire anguish fraught,
Unequal to sustain
The stress of that sore pain,
A twofold evil his rash spirit wrought.
First, with the hand that smote his sire he reft
Himself of sight, his only comfort left :—

Then, with his children wroth,
He fiercely launched on both
A biting curse for their unfilial ways,—
How with steel-furnished hand
They should divide his land
And heritage in lapse of after days.
Even now the fear works strongly in my soul,
The Erinnys of that curse runs close upon her goal.

LEWIS CAMPBELL.

SEPTEM CONTRA THEBAS.

848—860.

τάδ᾽ αὐτόδηλα, προῦπτος ἀγγέλου λόγος·   ἐπῳδ.
διπλαῖ μέριμναι, διδυμάνορα
κάκ᾽ αὐτοφόνα, δίμοιρα
τέλεια τάδε πάθη. τί φῶ;
τί δ᾽ ἄλλο γ᾽ ἢ πόνοι πόνων,
δόμων ἐφέστιοι;
ἀλλὰ γόων, ὦ φίλαι, κατ᾽ οὖρον
ἐρέσσετ᾽ ἀμφὶ κρατὶ πόμπιμον χεροῖν
πίτυλον, ὃς αἰὲν δι᾽ Ἀχέροντ᾽ ἀμείβεται
τὰν ἄστονον, μελάγκροκον
ναύστολον θεωρίδα,
τὰν ἀστιβῆ Ἀπόλλωνι, τὰν ἀνάλιον,
πάνδοκον εἰς ἀφανῆ τε χέρσον.

SEPTEM CONTRA THEBAS.

848—860.

Now do our eyes behold
   The tidings which were told :
Twin fallen kings, twin perished hopes to mourn,
   The slayer, the slain,
The entangled doom forlorn
   And ruinous end of twain.
Say, is not sorrow, is not sorrow's sum
On home and hearthstone come ?
   O waft with sighs the sail from shore,
O smite the bosom, cadencing the oar
That rows beyond the rueful stream for aye
     To the far strand,
   The ship of souls, the dark,
   The unreturning bark
Whereon light never falls nor foot of Day,
Ev'n to the bourne of all, to the unbeholden land.

A. E. HOUSMAN.

PERSÆ.

65—138.

πεπέρακεν μὲν ὁ περσέπτολις ἤδη   στρ. αʹ.
βασίλειος στρατὸς εἰς ἀντίπορον γείτονα χώραν,
λινοδέσμῳ σχεδίᾳ πορθμὸν ἀμείψας
Ἀθαμαντίδος Ἕλλας,
πολύγομφον ὅδισμα
ζυγὸν ἀμφιβαλὼν αὐχένι πόντου.

πολυάνδρου δʼ Ἀσίας θούριος ἄρχων   ἀντ. αʹ.
ἐπὶ πᾶσαν χθόνα ποιμανόριον θεῖον ἐλαύνει
διχόθεν, πεζονόμοις ἔκ τε θαλάσσας,
ὀχυροῖσι πεποιθὼς
στυφέλοις ἐφέταις, χρυ-
σογόνου γενεᾶς ἰσόθεος φώς.

κυανοῦν δʼ ὄμμασι λεύσσων φονίου δέργμα δράκοντος,   στρ. βʹ.
πολύχειρ καὶ πολυναύτης, Σύριόν θʼ ἅρμα διώκων,
ἐπάγει δουρικλύτοις ἀνδράσι τοξόδαμνον Ἄρη.

δόκιμος δʼ οὔτις ὑποστὰς μεγάλῳ ῥεύματι φωτῶν   ἀντ. βʹ.
ὀχυροῖς ἕρκεσιν εἴργειν ἄμαχον κῦμα θαλάσσας·
ἀπρόσοιστος γὰρ ὁ Περσῶν στρατὸς ἀλκίφρων τε λαός.

δολόμητιν δʼ ἀπάταν θεοῦ τίς ἀνὴρ θνατὸς ἀλύξει;   μεσῳδ.
τίς ὁ κραιπνῷ ποδὶ πηδήματος εὐπετοῦς ἀνάσσων;
†φιλόφρων γὰρ παρασαίνει βροτὸν
τόθεν οὐκ ἔστιν ὑπὲρ θνατὸν ἀλύξαντα φυγεῖν.

PERSÆ.

65—138.

ALREADY hath the royal host,
Spoiler of cities, gained the adverse coast ;
O'er cordage-fastened raft the channel they
    Of Athamantid Hellè passed,
    What time their many-bolted way
On the sea's neck, for servile yoke, they cast.

    Thus the fierce king who holds command
O'er populous Asia, drives through all the land
In twofold armament his flock divine,
    Land troops and those who stem the brine ;
    Strong in his stalwart captains, he
Of gold-born race the god-like progeny.

From eyes like deadly dragon's, flashing a lurid gleam,
With men and galleys countless, he drives his Syrian car,
'Gainst spear-famed warriors leading his arrow-puissant
      war.

And none of valour proven against the mighty stream
May stand a living bulwark, and that fierce billow stem ;
For Persia's host resistless is, and her stout-hearted men.

But ah ! what mortal baffle may
    A god's deep-plotted snare,—
Who may o'erleap with foot so light ?
    Atè at first, with semblance fair,
Into her toils allures her prey,
    Whence no mere mortal wight
      May break away.

θεόθεν ᵧαρ κατὰ μοῖρ᾽   στρ. ᵧ´.
ἐκράτηϑεν τὸ παλαι-
ὸν, ἐπέϑκηψε δὲ Πέρϑαις
πολέμους πυρᵧοᵟαίκτους
διέπειν ἱππιοχάρμας
τε κλόνους,
πύλεών τ᾽ ἀναϑτάϑεις.

ἔμαθον δ᾽ εὐρυπόροι-   ἀντ. ᵧ´.
υ θαλάϑϑας πολιαι-
νομένας πνεύματι λάβρῳ
ἐϑορᾶν πόντιον ἄλϑος,
πίϑυνοι λεπτοδώμοις πείϑ-
μαϑι λα-
υπόροις τε μηχαναῖς.

ταῦτά μου μελαγχίτων   στρ. δ´.
φρὴν ἀμύϑϑεται φόβῳ,
ὐά, Περϑικοῦ στρατεύματος
τοῦδε, μὴ πόλις πύθη-
ται κένανδρον μέᵧ᾽ ἄϑτυ Σουϑίδος·

καὶ τὸ Κιϑϑίων πόλιϑμ᾽   ἀντ. δ´.
ἀντίδουπον ἄϑεται,
ὐά, τοῦτ᾽ ἔπος ᵧυναικοπλη-
θὴς ὅμιλος ἀπύων·
βυϑϑίνοις δ᾽ ἐν πέπλοις πέϑῃ λακίς.

πᾶς ᵧὰρ ἱππηλάτας   στρ. ε´.
καὶ πεδοϑτιβὴς λεώς
ϑμῆνος ὡς ἐκλέλοι-
πεν μελιϑϑᾶν σὺν ὀρχάμῳ στρατοῦ,
τὸν ἀμφίζευκτον ἐξαμείψας
ἀμφοτέρας ἅλιον
πρῶνα κοινὸν αἴας.

In olden time by Heaven's decree
Fixed was the Persians' destiny ;—
Tower-battering war was theirs by Fate,
The turmoil when steed-mounted foes
In shock of battle fiercely close,
And cities to make desolate.

Now have they learned firm gaze to cast
On the vext sea, what time the blast
Makes hoary its broad-furrowed plain ;
Confide they now in naval craft,
Cables fine-wove, device to waft
      Armies across the main.

Hence, swartly robed, my heart by fear
Is tortured, lest ere long the state—
Woe for the Persian army !—hear
That Susa's mighty fort is desolate.

And Kissia's stronghold shall reply
Beat unto beat on doleful breast,
While crowds of women raise the cry,
Woe ! woe ! and rend their flaxen-tissued vest.

    For all the troops that draw the rein,
    And all who tread the dusty plain,
    Like swarming bees, with him who led
    Their martial host, abroad have sped,
    The bridge-joined headlands crossing o'er,
Washed by the sea, that links each adverse shore.

λέκτρα δ' ἀνδρῶν πόθῳ   ἀντ. ε'.
πίμπλαται δακρύμασιν·
Περσίδες δ' ἀκροπεν-
θεῖς ἑκάστα πόθῳ φιλάνορι
τὸν αἰχμάεντα θοῦρον εὐνα-
τῆρα προπεμψαμένα
λείπεται μονόζυξ.

SUPPLICES.

85—101.

†εἰ θείη Διὸς εὖ παναληθῶς·   στρ. δ'.
Διὸς ἵμερος οὐκ εὐθήρατος ἐτύχθη.
πάντα τοι φλεγέθει
κἀν σκότῳ μελαίνᾳ ξὺν τύχᾳ
μερόπεσσι λαοῖς.

᾿πίπτει δ' ἀσφαλὲς οὐδ' ἐπὶ νώτῳ,   ἀντ. δ'.
κορυφᾷ Διὸς εἰ κρανθῇ πρᾶγμα τέλειον.
δαυλοὶ γὰρ πραπίδων
δάσκιοί τε τείνουσιν πόροι,
κατιδεῖν ἄφραστοι.

ἰάπτει δ' ἐλπίδων   στρ. ε'.
ἀφ' ὑψιπύργων πανώλεις βροτοὺς,
βίαν δ' οὔτιν' ἐξοπλίζει,
†τὰν ἄποινον δαιμονίων· ἥμενον ἄνω φρόνημά πως
αὐτόθεν ἐξέπραξεν ἔμπας, ἑδράνων, ἐφ' ἁγνῶν.

And yearning love with many a tear
The couch bedeweth, lone and drear ;
The wives of Persia, steeped in woe,
Lament, of their dear lords bereft ;
For her fierce spouse against the foe
Each sent spear-armed, and mourns unmated left.

ANNA SWANWICK.

SUPPLICES.

85—101.

LET highest in mind be most in might.
The choice of Zeus what charm may bind ?
His thought, 'mid Fate's mysterious night,
A growing blaze against the wind
Prevails :—whate'er the nations say,
His purpose holds its darkling way.

What thing his nod hath ratified
Stands fast, and moves with firm, sure tread,
Nor sways, nor swerves, nor starts aside.
A mazy thicket, hard to thread,
A labyrinth undiscovered still,
The far-drawn windings of his will.

Down from proud towers of hope
He throws infatuate men ;
Nor needs, to reach his boundless scope,
The undistressful pain
Of Godlike effort.   On his holy seat
He thinks, and all is done, even as him seems most meet.

LEWIS CAMPBELL.

AGAMEMNON.

105—257.

κύριός εἰμι θροεῖν ὅδιον κράτος αἴσιον ἀνδρῶν   στρ. ά.
ἐκτελέων. ἔτι ζὰρ θεόθεν καταπνείει
πειθὼ μολπᾶν,
†ἀλκᾷ σύμφυτος αἰών,
ὅπως Ἀχαιῶν δίθρονον κράτος, Ἑλλάδος ἥβας
ξύμφρονα ταζάν,
πέμπει ξὺν δορὶ καὶ χερὶ πράκτορι
θούριος ὄρνις Τευκρίδ᾽ ἐπ᾽ αἶαν,
οἰωνῶν βασιλεὺς βασιλεῦσι νεῶν, ὁ κελαινὸς,
ὅ τ᾽ ἐξόπιν ἀρζᾶς,
φανέντες ἴκταρ μελάθρων, χερὸς ἐκ δοριπάλτου,
πιμπρέπτοις ἐν ἕδραισι,
βοσκόμενοι λαζίναν ἐρικύμονα φέρματι ζένναν,
βλαβέντα λοισθίων δρόμων.
αἴλινον αἴλινον εἰπέ, τὸ δ᾽ εὖ νικάτω.

κεδνὸς δὲ στρατόμαντις ἰδὼν δύο λήμασι πιστοὺς   ἀντ. ά.
Ἀτρεΐδας μαχίμους, ἐδάη λαζοδαίτας
πομπούς τ᾽ ἀρχάς·
οὕτω δ᾽ εἶπε τεράζων·
χρόνῳ μὲν ἀζρεῖ Πριάμου πόλιν ἅδε κέλευθος,
πάντα δὲ πύρζων
κτήνη πρόσθε τὰ δημιοπληθῆ
Μοῖρ᾽ ἀλαπάξει πρὲς τὸ βίαιον.
οἶον μή τις ἄζα θεόθεν κνεφάσῃ προτυπὲν στόμ-
ιον μέζα Τροίας
στρατωθέν. οἴκῳ γὰρ ἐπίφθονος Ἄρτεμις ἁζνὰ,
πτανοῖσιν κυσὶ πατρὸς,
αὐτότοκον πρὸ λόχου μοζερὰν πτάκα θυομένοισι·
στυζεῖ δὲ δεῖπνον αἰετῶν.
αἴλινον αἴλινον εἰπέ, τὸ δ᾽ εὖ νικάτω.

AGAMEMNON.

105—257.

POWER is upon me now, to sing the awful sign
   That crossed the warrior monarchs on their road ;
Heaven breathes within the 'suasive song divine,
   And strength through my rapt soul is pour'd abroad.
      The birds I sing, whose fateful flight
      Sent forth the twin-throned Argive might,
And all the youth of Greece, a gallant crew,
      With spear in each avenging hand,
      Against the guilty Trojan land.
Even at the threshold of the palace, flew
      The king of birds o'er either king,
      One black, and one with snow-white wing,
Right-ward, on the hand that grasps the spear,
Down through the glittering courts they steer,
      Swooping the hare's prolific brood,
      No more to crop its grassy food.
Ring out the dolorous hymn, yet triumph still the good !

But the wise seer, in his prophetic view—
   When he the twin-soul'd sons of Atreus saw,
At once the feasters on the hares he knew,   [awe :—
   Those leaders of the host, then broke his words of
" In time old Priam's city wall
   Before that conquering host shall fall,
   And all within her towers lie waste ;
   Her teeming wealth of man and beast
   Shall Fate in her dire violence destroy ;
   May ne'er heaven's envy, like a cloud,
   So darken o'er that army proud,
      The fine-forged curb of Troy !
   For Artemis, with jealous ire,
   Beholds the wingèd hounds of her great sire
   Swooping the innocent leverets' scarce-born brood,
   And loathes the eagles' feast of blood.
Ring out the dolorous hymn, yet triumph still the good !

τόσον περ εὔφρων ἁ καλὰ   μεσῳδ.
δρύζοισιν ἀέπτοις μαλερῶν λεόντων,
πάντων τ' ἀγρονόμων φιλομάστοις
θηρῶν ὀβρικάλοισι, τερπνὰ
τούτων αἰτεῖ ξύμβολα κρᾶναι,
δεξιὰ μέν, κατάμομφα δὲ φάζματα στρουθῶν.
ἰήιον δὲ καλέω Παιᾶνα,
μή τινας ἀντιπνόους Δαναοῖς χρονίας ἐχενῇδας
ἀπλοίας τεύξῃ,
σπευδομένα θυζίαν ἑτέραν, ἄνομόν τιν', ἄδαιτον,
νεικέων τέκτονα σύμφυτον,
οὐ δειζήνορα. μίμνει γὰρ φοβερὰ παλίνορτος
οἰκονόμος δολία, μνάμων μῆνις τεκνόποινος.
τοιάδε Κάλχας ξὺν μεγάλοις ἀγαθοῖς ἀπέκλαγξε
μόρζιμ' ἀπ' ὀρνίθων ὁδίων οἴκοις βασιλείοις·
τοῖς δ' ὁμόφωνον
αἴλινον αἴλινον εἰπέ, τὸ δ' εὖ νικάτω.

Ζεὺς, ὅζτις ποτ' ἐστίν, εἰ τόδ' αὐ-   στρ. β'.
τῷ φίλον κεκλημένῳ,
τοῦτό νιν προζεννέπω.
οὐκ ἔχω προζεικάζαι,
πάντ' ἐπισταθμώμενος,
πλὴν Διὸς, εἰ τὸ μάταν ἀπὸ φροντίδος ἄχθος
χρὴ βαλεῖν ἐτητύμως.

οὐδ' ὅζτις πάροιθεν ἦν μέγας,   ἀντ. β'.
παμμάχῳ θράζει βρύων,
οὐδὲν ἂν λέξαι πρὶν ὢν,
ὃς δ' ἔπειτ' ἔφυ, τρια-
κτῆρος οἴχεται τυχών.
Ζῆνα δέ τις προφρόνως ἐπινίκια κλάζων
τεύξεται φρενῶν τὸ πᾶν·

" Such is that beauteous Goddess' love
   To the strong lion's callow brood,
And all that the green meadows wont to rove,
   From the full udder quaff the liquid food.
O Goddess ! though thy wrath reprove
Those savage birds, yet turn those awful signs to good !"
   But, Io Pæan ! now I cry ;
   May ne'er her injured deity
   With adverse fleet-imprisoning blast
   The unpropitious sky o'ercast ;
      Hastening that other sacrifice—
   That darker sacrifice, unblest
   By music or by jocund feast :
      Whence sad domestic strife shall rise,
   And, dreadless of her lord, fierce woman's hate ;
   Whose child-avenging wrath in sullen state
   Broods, wily housewife, in her chamber's gloom,
      Over that unforgotten doom."
Such were the words that Calchas clanged abroad,
When crossed those ominous birds the onward road
   Of that twice royal brotherhood :
         A mingled doom
         Of glory and of gloom.
Ring out the dolorous hymn, yet triumph still the good !

   Whoe'er thou art, Great Power above,
   If that dread name thou best approve,
   All duly weighed I cannot find,
   Unburthening my o'erloaded mind,
   A mightier name than that of mightiest Jove.

   He, that so great of old
Branched out in strength invincible and bold,
   Is nothing now.   Who after came,
   Before the victor sank to shame :
Most wise is he who sings the all-conquering might of
   Jove—

τὸν φρονεῖν βροτοὺς ὁδώ-   στρ. ϛ΄.
σαντα, τὸν πάθει μάθος
θέντα κυρίως ἔχειν.
στάζει δ᾽ ἔν θ᾽ ὕπνῳ πρὸ καρδίας
μνησιπήμων πόνος· καὶ παρ᾽ ἄ-
κοντας ἦλθε σωφρονεῖν.
δαιμόνων δέ που χάρις,
βιαίως σέλμα σεμνὸν ἡμένων.

καὶ τόθ᾽ ἡγεμὼν ὁ πρές-   ἀντ. ϛ΄.
βυς νεῶν Ἀχαιϊκῶν,
μάντιν οὔτινα ψέγων,
ἐμπαίοις τύχαισι συμπνέων,
εὖτ᾽ ἀπλοίᾳ κεναγγεῖ βαρύ-
νοντ᾽ Ἀχαιϊκὸς λεώς,
Χαλκίδος πέραν ἔχων
παλιρρύχθοις ἐν Αὐλίδος τόποις.

πνοαὶ δ᾽ ἀπὸ Στρυμόνος μολοῦσαι   στρ. δ΄.
κακόσχολοι, νήστιδες, δύσορμοι
βροτῶν ἄλαι, νεῶν τε καὶ πεισμάτων ἀφειδεῖς,
παλιμμήκη χρόνον τιθεῖσαι
τρίβῳ, κατέξαινον ἄνθος Ἀργείων.
ἐπεὶ δὲ καὶ πικροῦ
χείματος ἄλλο μῆχαρ
βριθύτερον πρύμοισιν
μάντις ἔκλαγξεν, προφέρων Ἄρτεμιν, ὥστε χθόνα βά-
κτροις ἐπικρούσαντας Ἀτρείδας δάκρυ μὴ κατασχεῖν.

Jove, that great God
Who taught to mortals wisdom's road ;
   By whose eternal rule
Adversity is grave instruction's school.
   In the calm hour of sleep
Conscience, the sad remembrancer, will creep
To the inmost heart, and there enforce
On the reluctant spirit the wisdom of remorse.
   Mighty the grace of those dread deities,
Throned on their judgment bench, high in the empyrean
     skies !

Nor then did the elder chief, in sooth,
     Of all the Achean youth,
Dare brand with blame the holy seer ;
When adverse fortune 'gan to veer,
Emprisoning that becalmèd host
     On Chalcis' coast,
Where the heavy refluent billows roar
'Gainst Aulis' rock-bound shore.

And long and long from wintry Strymon blew
   The weary, hungry, anchor-straining blasts,
The winds that wandering seamen dearly rue,
   Nor spared the cables worn, and groaning masts ;
And, lingering on in indolent delay,
Slow wasted all the strength of Greece away.
But when the shrill-voiced prophet 'gan proclaim
   That remedy more dismal and more dread
   Than the drear weather blackening overhead ;
And spoke in Artemis' most awful name,
The sons of Atreus, 'mid their armèd peers,
Their sceptres dashed to earth, and each broke out in
     tears.

ἄναξ δ' ὁ πρέσβυς τότ' εἶπε φωνῶν·   ἀντ. δ΄.
βαρεῖα μὲν κὴρ τὸ μὴ πιθέσθαι,
βαρεῖα δ', εἰ τέκνον δαΐξω, δόμων ἄγαλμα,
μιαίνων παρθενοσφάγοισι
ῥείθροις πατρῴους χέρας βωμοῦ πέλας.
τί τῶνδ' ἄνευ κακῶν;
πῶς λιπόναυς γένωμαι,
ξυμμαχίας ἁμαρτών;
παυσανέμου γὰρ θυσίας παρθενίου θ' αἵματος ὀρ-
γᾷ περιόργως ἐπιθυμεῖν θέμις. εὖ γὰρ εἴη.

ἐπεὶ δ' ἀνάγκας ἔδυ λέπαδνον   στρ. ε΄.
φρενὸς πνέων δυσσεβῆ τροπαίαν
ἄναγνον, ἀνίερον, τόθεν
τὸ παντότολμον φρονεῖν μετέγνω.
βροτοὺς θρασύνει γὰρ αἰσχρόμητις
τάλαινα παρακοπὰ
πρωτοπήμων. ἔτλα δ' οὖν
θυτὴρ γενέσθαι θυγατρὸς γυναικοποίνων πολέμων ἀρωγὰν
καὶ προτέλεια ναῶν·

λιτὰς δὲ καὶ κληδόνας πατρῴους   ἀντ. ε΄.
παρ' οὐδὲν αἰῶνα παρθένειόν τ'
ἔθεντο φιλόμαχοι βραβῆς,
φράσεν δ' ἀόζοις πατὴρ μετ' εὐχὰν,
δίκαν χιμαίρας ὕπερθε βωμοῦ
πέπλοισι περιπετῆ,
παντὶ θυμῷ προνωπῆ
λαβεῖν ἀέρδην, στόματός τε καλλιπρῴρου φυλακὰν κατασχεῖν,
φθόγγον ἀραῖον οἴκοις,

And thus the elder king began to say :
" Dire doom ! to disobey the Gods' command !
More dire, my child, mine house's pride, to slay,
    Dabbling in virgin blood a father's hands.
    Alas ! alas ! which way to fly ?
    As base deserter quit the host,
    The pride and strength of our great league all lost ?
Should I the storm-appeasing rite deny,
Will not their wrathfullest wrath rage up and swell—
Exact the virgin's blood ?—oh, would 'twere o'er and
    well ! "

So 'neath Necessity's stern yoke he passed,
    And his lost soul, with impious impulse veering,
Surrendered to the accurst unholy blast,
    Warped to the dire extreme of human daring.
        The frenzy of affliction still
        Maddens, dire counsellor, man's soul to ill.
So he endured to be the priest
In that child-slaughtering rite unblest,
    The first-fruit offering of that host
    In fatal war for a bad woman lost.
The prayers, the mute appeal to her hard sire,
        Her youth, her virgin beauty,
Nought heeded they, the chiefs for war on fire.
        So to the ministers of that dire duty
(First having prayed) the father gave the sign,
Like some soft kid, to lift her to the shrine.
    There lay she prone,
Her graceful garments round her thrown ;
But first her beauteous mouth around
    Their violent bonds they wound,
Lest her dread curse the fated house should smite
With their rude inarticulate might.

†βίᾳ χαλινῶν δ' ἀναύδῳ μένει   στρ. ζ'.
κρόκου βαφὰς ἐς πέδον χέουσα
ἔβαλλ' ἕκαστον θυτήρων ἀπ' ὄμματος βέλει φιλοίκτῳ,
πρέπουσά θ' ὡς ἐν γραφαῖς, προσεννέπειν
θέλουσ', ἐπεὶ πολλάκις
πατρὸς κατ' ἀνδρῶνας εὐτραπέζους
ἔμελψεν. ἁγνὰ δ' ἀταύρωτος αὐδᾷ πατρὸς
φίλου τριτόσπονδον εὔποτμόν τ'
αἰῶνα φίλως ἐτίμα.

τὰ δ' ἔνθεν οὔτ' εἶδον οὔτ' ἐννέπω·   ἀντ. ζ'.
τέχναι δὲ Κάλχαντος οὐκ ἄκραντοι.
δίκα δὲ τοῖς μὲν παθοῦσιν μαθεῖν ἐπιρρέπει τὸ μέλλον.
τὸ δὲ προκλύειν, ἐπεὶ γένοιτ' ἂν ἤλυσις, προχαιρέτω·
ἴσον δὲ τῷ προστένειν.
τορὸν γὰρ ἥξει σύνορθρον αὐγαῖς.
πέλοιτο δ' οὖν τἀπὶ τούτοισιν εὔπραξις, ὡς
θέλει τόδ' ἄγχιστον Ἀπίας
γαίας μονόφρουρον ἕρκος.

But she her saffron robe to earth let fall :
　The shaft of pity from her eye
Transpierced that awful priesthood—one and all.
　Lovely as in a picture stood she by
As she would speak.　Thus at her father's feasts
The virgin, 'mid the revelling guests,
Was wont with her chaste voice to supplicate
For her dear father an auspicious fate.

　I saw no more ! to speak more is not mine ;
Not unfulfilled was Chalcas' lore divine.
　　　Eternal justice still will bring
　　　Wisdom out of suffering.
So to the fond desire farewell,
The inevitable future to foretell ;
　'Tis but our woe to antedate ;
Joint knit with joint, expands the full-formed fate.
　Yet at the end of these dark days
May prospering weal return at length ;
　Thus in his spirit prays
He of the Apian land the sole remaining strength.

DEAN MILMAN.

AGAMEMNON.

160—183.

Ζεὺς, ὅστις ποτ᾽ ἐστίν, εἰ τόδ᾽ αὐ-　　　στρ. β'.
τῷ φίλον κεκλημένῳ,
τοῦτό νιν προσεννέπω.
οὐκ ἔχω προσεικάσαι,
πάντ᾽ ἐπισταθμώμενος,
πλὴν Διός, εἰ τὸ μάταν ἀπὸ φροντίδος ἄχθος
χρὴ βαλεῖν ἐτητύμως.

οὐδ᾽ ὅστις πάροιθεν ἦν μέγας,　　　ἀντ. β'.
παμμάχῳ θράσει βρύων,
οὐδὲν ἂν λέξαι πρὶν ὤν,
ὃς δ᾽ ἔπειτ᾽ ἔφυ, τρια-
κτῆρος οἴχεται τυχών.
Ζῆνα δέ τις προφρόνως ἐπινίκια κλάζων
τεύξεται φρενῶν τὸ πᾶν·

τὸν φρονεῖν βροτοὺς ὁδώ-　　　στρ. γ'.
σαντα, τὸν πάθει μάθος
θέντα κυρίως ἔχειν.
στάζει δ᾽ ἔν θ᾽ ὕπνῳ πρὸ καρδίας
μνησιπήμων πόνος· καὶ παρ᾽ ἄ-
κοντας ἦλθε σωφρονεῖν.
δαιμόνων δέ που χάρις,
βιαίως σέλμα σεμνὸν ἡμένων.

AGAMEMNON.

160—183.

ZEUS, whosoe'er he be, if this name please his ear,
By this name I bid him hear :
Nought but Zeus my soul may guess,
Seeking far and seeking near,
Seeking who shall stay the stress
Of its fond and formless fear.
For He who long ago was great,
Filled with daring and with might,
Now is silent, lost in night :
And the next that took his state
Met his supplanter too, and fell, and sank from sight.

Zeus Victorious hail we then,
Zeus that leadeth souls of men—
Thus his deep decrees ordain—
To Wisdom's goal o'er the drear road of Pain.
In sleep there doth before the heart distil
A grievous memory of ill,
Making the unwise wise against his will.
So unto Man, in kind compulsion given,
Falls the high grace of Gods from awful thrones of
    Heaven.

ERNEST MYERS.

AGAMEMNON.

355—474.

ὦ Ζεῦ βασιλεῦ καὶ νὺξ φιλία
μεγάλων κόσμων κτεάτειρα,
ἥτ' ἐπὶ Τροίας πύργοις ἔβαλες
στεγανὸν δίκτυον, ὡς μήτε μέγαν
μήτ' οὖν νεαρῶν τιν' ὑπερτελέσαι
μέγα δουλείας
γάγγαμον, ἄτης παναλώτου.
Δία τοι ξένιον μέγαν αἰδοῦμαι
τὸν τάδε πράξαντ', ἐπ' Ἀλεξάνδρῳ
τείνοντα πάλαι τόξον, ὅπως ἂν
μήτε πρὸ καιροῦ μήθ' ὑπὲρ ἄστρων
βέλος ἠλίθιον σκήψειεν.

Διὸς πλαγὰν ἔχουσιν εἰπεῖν,   στρ. α'.
πάρεστι τοῦτό γ' ἐξιχνεῦσαι.
ἔπραξεν ὡς ἔκρανεν. οὐκ ἔφα τις
θεοὺς βροτῶν ἀξιοῦσθαι μέλειν
ὅσοις ἀθίκτων χάρις
πατοῖθ' · ὁ δ' οὐκ εὐσεβής.
πέφανται δ' ἐκγόνους
ἀτολμήτων Ἄρη
πνεόντων μεῖζον ἢ δικαίως,

AGAMEMNON.

355—474.

ZEUS, Lord of Heaven ! and welcome Night
Of victory, that hast our might
    With all the glories crowned !
On towers of Ilion, free no more,
Hast flung the mighty mesh of war,
    And closely girt them round,
Till neither warrior may 'scape,
Nor stripling lightly overleap
The trammels as they close, and close,
Till with the grip of doom our foes
    In slavery's coil are bound !
Zeus, Lord of Hospitality !
In grateful awe I bend to thee—
    'Tis thou hast struck the blow !
    At Alexander, long ago,
    We marked thee bend thy vengeful bow,
But long and warily withhold
The eager shaft, which, uncontrolled
And loosed too soon or launched too high,
Had wandered bloodless thro' the sky !

Zeus, the high God !—whate'er be dim in doubt,
    This can our thought track out—
The blow that fells the sinner is of God,
    And as he wills, the rod
Of vengeance smiteth sore.   One said of old,
    " The Gods list not to hold
A reckoning with him whose feet oppress
    The grace of holiness "—
An impious word ! for whensoe'er the sire
    Breathed forth rebellious fire—

φλεόντων δωμάτων ὑπέρφευ
ὑπὲρ τὸ βέλτιστον. ἔστω δ᾽ ἀπή-
μαντον, ὥστε κἀπαρκεῖν
εὖ πραπίδων λαχόντα.
οὐ γάρ ἐστιν ἔπαλξις
πλούτου πρὸς κόρον ἀνδρὶ
λακτίσαντι μέγαν δίκας
βωμὸν εἰς ἀφάνειαν.

βιᾶται δ᾽ ἁ τάλαινα πειθώ,   ἀντ. ά.
προβουλόπαις ἄφερτος ἄτας.
ἄκος δὲ πᾶν μάταιον. οὐκ ἐκρύφθη,
πρέπει δέ, φῶς αἰνολαμπές, σίνος·
κακοῦ δὲ χαλκοῦ τρόπον
τρίβῳ τε καὶ προσβολαῖς
μελαμπαγὴς πέλει
δικαιωθείς, ἐπεὶ
διώκει παῖς ποτανὸν ὄρνιν,
πόλει πρόστριμμ᾽ ἄφερτον ἐνθείς.
λιτᾶν δ᾽ ἀκούει μὲν οὔτις θεῶν·
τὸν δ᾽ ἐπίστροφον τῶνδε
φῶτ᾽ ἄδικον καθαιρεῖ.
οἷος καὶ Πάρις ἐλθὼν
ἐς δόμον τὸν Ἀτρειδᾶν
ᾔσχυνε ξενίαν τράπε-
ζαν κλοπαῖσι γυναικός.

λιποῦσα δ᾽ ἀστοῖσιν ἀσπίστορας   στρ. β'.
κλόνους λογχίμους τε καὶ ναυβάτας ὁπλισμούς,
ἄγουσά τ᾽ ἀντίφερνον Ἰλίῳ φθοράν,
βέβακεν ῥίμφα διὰ πυλᾶν,

What time his household overflowed the measure
    Of bliss and health and treasure—
His children's children read the reckoning plain,
    At last, in tears and pain !
On me let weal that brings no woe be sent,
    And therewithal, content ;
Who spurns the shrine of Right, nor wealth nor power
    Shall be to him a tower,
To guard him from the gulf : there lies his lot,
    Where all things are forgot !

Lust drives him on—lust, desperate and wild,
    Fate's sin-contriving child—
And cure is none ; beyond concealment clear,
    Kindles Sin's baleful glare.
As an ill coin beneath the wearing touch
    Betrays, by stain and smutch,
Its metal false—such is the sinful wight.
    Before, on pinions light,
Fair Pleasure flits, and lures him childlike on,
    While home and kin make moan,
Beneath the grinding burden of his crime ;
    Till, in the end of time,
Cast down of heaven, he pours forth fruitless prayer,
    To Powers that will not hear.
    And such did Paris come
    Unto Atrides' home,
And thence, with sin and shame his welcome to repay,
    Ravished the wife away—

And she, unto her country and her kin
Leaving the clash of shields and spears and arming ships,
And bearing unto Troy destruction for a dower,
    And overbold in sin,
Went fleetly through the gates, at midnight hour.

ἄτλητα τλᾶσα· πολλὰ δ᾽ ἔστενον
τόδ᾽ ἐννέποντες δόμων προφῆται·
ἰὼ ἰὼ δῶμα δῶμα καὶ πρόμοι,
ἰὼ λέχος καὶ στίβοι φιλάνορες.
† πάρεστι σιγᾶσ᾽, ἄτιμος, ἀλοίδορος,
ἄδιστος ἀφεμένων ἰδεῖν.
πόθῳ δ᾽ ὑπερποντίας
φάσμα δόξει δόμων ἀνάσσειν.
εὐμόρφων δὲ κολοσσῶν
ἔχθεται χάρις ἀνδρί.
ὀμμάτων δ᾽ ἐν ἀχηνίαις
ἔρρει πᾶσ᾽ Ἀφροδίτα.

ὀνειρόφαντοι δὲ πενθήμονες   ἀντ. β΄.
πάρεισιν δοκαὶ φέρουσαι χάριν ματαίαν.
μάταν γὰρ εὖτ᾽ ἂν ἐσθλά τις δοκῶν ὁρᾶν,
παραλλάξασα διὰ χερῶν,
βέβακεν ὄψις οὐ μεθύστερον
πτεροῖς ὀπαδοῖς ὕπνου κελεύθοις.
τὰ μὲν κατ᾽ οἴκους ἐφ᾽ ἑστίας ἄχη
τάδ᾽ ἐστὶ καὶ τῶνδ᾽ ὑπερβατώτερα.
τὸ πᾶν δ᾽ ἀφ᾽ Ἑλλάδος αἴας συνορμένοις
πένθεια τλησικάρδιος
δόμων ἑκάστου πρέπει.

πολλὰ γοῦν θιγγάνει πρὸς ἧπαρ·
οὓς μὲν γάρ τις ἔπεμψεν
οἶδεν· ἀντὶ δὲ φωτῶν
τεύχη καὶ σποδὸς εἰς ἑκά-
στου δόμους ἀφικνεῖται.

Oft, from the prophets' lips,
Moaned out the warning and the wail—Ah woe!
Woe for the home, the home! and for the chieftains,
   Woe for the bride-bed, warm   [woe!
Yet from the lovely limbs, the impress of the form
    Of her who loved her lord, awhile ago!
      And woe for him who stands
Shamed, silent, unreproachful, stretching hands
    That find her not, and sees, yet will not see,
      That she is far away!
And his sad fancy, yearning o'er the sea,
    Shall summon and recall
Her wraith, once more to queen it in his hall.
    And sad with many memories,
The fair cold beauty of each sculptured face—
    And all to hatefulness is turned their grace,
Seen blankly by forlorn and hungering eyes!
    And when the night is deep,
Come visions, sweet and sad, and bearing pain
    Of hopings vain—
Void, void and vain, for scarce the sleeping sight
    Has seen its old delight,
When thro' the grasps of love that bid it stay
    It vanishes away
On silent wings that roam adown the ways of Sleep!

    Such are the sights, the sorrows fell,
About our hearth—and worse, whereof I may not tell.
    But, all the wide town o'er,
Each home that sent its master far away
    From Hellas' shore
Feels the keen thrill of heart, the pang of loss, to-day;
    For, truth to say,
The touch of bitter death is manifold!
Familiar was each face, and dear as life,
    That went unto the war,

ὁ χρυσαμοιβὸς δ᾽ Ἄρης σωμάτων   στρ. γ᾽.
καὶ ταλαντοῦχος ἐν μάχῃ δορὸς
πυρωθὲν ἰξ Ἰλίου
φίλοισι πέμπει βαρυ
ψῆγμα δυσδάκρυτον ἀν-
τήνορος σποδοῦ γεμί-
ζων λέβητας εὐθέτου.
στένουσι δ᾽ εὖ λέγοντες ἄν-
δρα τὸν μὲν ὡς μάχης ἴδρις·
τὸν δ᾽ ἐν φοναῖς καλῶς πεσόντ᾽
ἀλλοτρίας διαὶ γυναικός.
τάδε σῖγά τις βαΰζει.
φθονερὸν δ᾽ ὑπ᾽ ἄλγος ἕρπει
προδίκοις Ἀτρείδαις.
οἱ δ᾽ αὐτοῦ περὶ τεῖχος
θήκας Ἰλιάδος γᾶς
εὔμορφοι κατέχουσιν· ἐχ-
θρὰ δ᾽ ἔχοντας ἔκρυψεν.

βαρεῖα δ᾽ ἀστῶν φάτις ξὺν κότῳ·   ἀντ. γ᾽.
δημοκράντου δ᾽ ἀρᾶς τίνει χρέος.
μένει δ᾽ ἀκοῦσαί τί μου
μέριμνα νυκτηρεφές.

But thither, whence a warrior went of old,
    Doth nought return,
Only a spear and sword, and ashes in an urn !
    For Ares, lord of strife,
Who doth the swaying scales of battle hold,
War's money-changer, giving dust for gold,
    Sends back, to hearts that held them dear,
Scant ash of warriors, wept with many a tear,
Light to the hand, but heavy to the soul ;
    Yea, fills the light urn full
    With what survived the flame—
Death's dusty measure of a hero's frame !

"Alas !" one cries, "and yet alas again !
Our chief is gone, the hero of the spear,
    And has not left his peer !"
"Ah woe !" another moans—" my spouse is slain,
    The death of honour, rolled in dust and blood,
Slain for a woman's sin, a false wife's shame !"
    Such muttered words of bitter mood
Rise against those who went forth to reclaim ;
Yea, jealous wrath creeps on, against th' Atrides' name !
    And others, far beneath the Ilian wall,
Sleep their last sleep—the goodly chiefs and tall,
    Couched in the foeman's land, whereon they gave
Their breath, and lords of Troy, each in his Trojan
    grave !

Therefore, for each and all, the city's breast
Is heavy with a wrath supprest,
As deep and deadly as a curse more loud
    Flung by the common crowd :
And, brooding deeply, doth my soul await
    Tidings of coming fate,
Buried as yet in darkness' womb.

τῶν πολυκτόνων γὰρ οὐκ
ἄσκοποι θεοί. κελαι-
ναὶ δ' Ἐρινύες χρόνῳ
τυχηρὸν ὄντ' ἄνευ δίκας,
παλιντυχεῖ τριβᾷ βίου
τιθεῖσ' ἀμαυρὸν, ἐν δ' ἀΐ-
στοις τελέθοντος οὔτις ἀλκά·
τὸ δ' ὑπερκόπως κλύειν εὖ
βαρύ· βάλλεται γὰρ ὄσσοις
διόθεν κεραυνός.
κρίνω δ' ἄφθονον ὄλβον.
μήτ' εἴην πτολιπόρθης
μήτ' οὖν αὐτὸς ἁλοὺς ὑπ' ἄλλων βίον κατίδοιμι.

AGAMEMNON.

681—781.

τίς ποτ' ὠνόμαζεν ὧδ'   στρ. α'.
ἐς τὸ πᾶν ἐτητύμως—
μή τις ὅντιν' οὐχ ὁρῶ-
μεν προνοίαισι τοῦ πεπρωμένου
γλῶσσαν ἐν τύχᾳ νέμων;—
τὰν δορίγαμβρον ἀμφινεικῆ θ' Ἑλέναν;
ἐπεὶ πρεπόντως
ἑλέναυς, ἕλανδρος, ἑλέπτολις,
ἐκ τῶν ἁβροπήνων
προκαλυμμάτων ἔπλευσε

For not forgetful is the high Gods' doom,
    Against the sons of carnage : all too long
Seems the unjust to prosper and be strong,
    Till the dark Furies come,
And smite with stern reversal all his home,
    Down into dim obstruction—he is gone,
And help and hope, among the Lost, is none.
O'er him who vaunteth an exceeding fame
    Impends a woe condign ;
The vengeful bolt upon his eyes doth flame,
    Sped from the hand divine.
This bliss be mine, ungrudged of God to feel,
    To tread no city to the dust,
    Nor see my own life thrust
Down to a slave's estate beneath another's heel !

E. D. A. MORSHEAD.

AGAMEMNON.

681—781.

WHO gave the ill-omened name
So fraught with terror for the time to be,
    So true to her career of blame,—
War-wooed, war-won, war-wakening Helenè ?
Was he some prophet-spirit unknown to fame,
      With sure presentiment
      Fore-speaking Time's event ?
The name of Helen tells of ships a-flame,
      Of souls to Hades sent,
Of countries ravaged, cities overthrown !

ξεφύρου γίγαντος αὔρᾳ,
πολύανδροί τε φεράσπιδες
κυναγοὶ κατ' ἴχνος,
πλατᾶν ἄφαντον,
† κέλσαντες Σιμόεντος
ἀκτὰς ἐπ' ἀεξιφύλλους,
δι' ἔριν αἱματύεσσαν.

'Ιλίῳ δὲ κῆδος ὀρ-
θώνυμον τελεσσίφρων
μῆνις ἤλασεν, τραπέ-
ζας ἀτίμωσιν ὑστέρῳ χρόνῳ
καὶ ξυνεστίου Διὸς
πρασσομένα, τὸ νυμφότιμον μέλος ἐκ-
† φάτως τίοντος,
ὑμέναιον, ὃς τότ' ἐπέρρεπεν
γαμβροῖσιν εἴδειν.
μεταμανθάνουσα δ' ὕμνον
Πριάμου πόλις γεραιὰ
πολύθρηνον μέγα που στένει,
κικλήσκουσα Πάριν
τὸν αἰνόλεκτρον,
παμπρόσθη πολύθρηνον
αἰῶν' ἀμφὶ πολιτᾶν
μέλεον αἷμ' ἀνατλᾶσα.

From out the delicately curtained bower,
   Borne by the West Wind's earth-born power,
In Paris' nimble galley forth she went,
   And when they touched on Simoïs' shore
With cytisus and myrtle overgrown,
     A many-shielded pack,
     Following the viewless track
       Of their swift oar,
Came bent on slaughterous feud and fierce arbitrament.

That *bond*, so rightly styled,
Bound Ilion with a chain of endless care,
   Sent by some spirit of anger wild
Resolved on ruin, minded to prepare
Revenge for hospitality defiled
     On those who sang that day
     The lawless marriage lay,
Provoking wrath hard to be reconciled.
     Her new-found brethren gay
Thought not if Zeus approved the enforced song.

Now yonder choir hath conned a different strain,
   And Priam's ancient town with pain
Groans heavily from forth her ashes grey,
   Calling on Paris the accurst,
The guilty cause of unforgiven wrong ;—
     She, who in wild despair
     For generations fair
       Herself had nurst,
Hath spent an age of years in wailing midst the fray.

† ἔθρεψεν δὲ λέοντα   στρ. β΄.
σίνιν δόμοις ἀγάλακτον
οὕτως ἀνὴρ φιλόμαστον,
ἐν βιότου προτελείοις
ἅμερον, εὐφιλόπαιδα,
καὶ γεραροῖς ἐπίχαρτον.
πολέα δ᾽ ἔσχ᾽ ἐν ἀγκάλαις,
νεοτρόφου τέκνου δίκαν,
φαιδρωπὸς ποτὶ χεῖρα, σαί-
νων τε γαστρὸς ἀνάγκαις.

χρονισθεὶς δ᾽ ἀπέδειξεν   ἀντ. β΄.
ἔθος τὸ πρόσθε τοκήων.
χάριν τροφᾶς γὰρ ἀμείβων,
μηλοφόνοισιν ἄγαισιν
δαῖτ᾽ ἀκέλευστος ἔτευξεν·
αἵματι δ᾽ οἶκος ἐφύρθη·
ἄμαχον ἄλγος οἰκέταις,
μέγα σίνος πολυκτόνον.
ἐκ θεοῦ δ᾽ ἱερεύς τις ἄ-
τας δόμοις προσεθρέφθη.

παρ᾽ αὐτὰ δ᾽ ἐλθεῖν ἐς Ἰλίου πόλιν   στρ. γ΄.
λέγοιμ᾽ ἂν φρόνημα μὲν νηνέμου γαλάνας,
ἀκασκαῖον δ᾽ ἄγαλμα πλούτου,
μαλθακὸν ὀμμάτων βέλος,
δηξίθυμον ἔρωτος ἄνθος.

What image fits Troy's fall?
   A man, I will say,
   Cherished within his hall
   A cub, for play,
Just weaned, but hardly, from the lioness.
   The prelude of his life
   Was far from cruel strife ;—
The darling of young boys, a thing of sportiveness.
   Even old men felt the charm :
   Oft in the nestling arm
'Twas dandled, like to human babyhood ;
   When stroked, he made reply
   With fondly brightening eye :
When hunger pressed, he crouched, and fawned for food.

   But as with time he grew
   He showed his stock,
   And with dire outrage slew
   The home-bred flock,—
So making vile return for all that care ;—
   Till all the peaceful floor
   With blood was dabbled o'er.
The household slaves beheld in mute despair.
   The self-provided feast
   Of that unbidden guest
Spread havoc round him wheresoe'er he moved.
   Sent by some God to Earth
   To plague a sinful hearth,
A priest of Atè's self that nursling proved.

Even so, methinks, there came to Troia's town
   A spirit like the calm on windless seas,
A face to smite the soul, but ne'er to frown,
   A joy luxurious, crowning wealth with ease.
Love there in bloom entranced the passionate mind.

† παρακλίνουσ' ἐπέκρανεν
δὲ ϝάμου πικρὰς τελευτὰς,
δύσεδρος καὶ δυσόμιλος
συμένα Πριαμίδαισιν,
πομπᾷ Διὸς ξενίου,
νυμφόκλαυτος 'Ερινύς.

π002 παλαίφατος δ' ἐν βροτοῖς ϝέρων λόϝος   ἀντ. ϝ'.
τέτυκται, μεϝὰν τελεσθέντα φωτὸς ὄλβον
τεκνοῦσθαι μηδ' ἄπαιδα θνήσκειν,
ἐκ δ' ἀϝαθᾶς τύχας ϝένει
βλαστάνειν ἀκόρεστον οἰζύν.
δίχα δ' ἄλλων μονόφρων εἰ-
μί. τὸ δυσσεβὲς ϝὰρ ἔρϝον
μετὰ μὲν πλείονα τίκτει,
σφετέρᾳ δ' εἰκότα ϝέννᾳ.
οἴκων δ' ἄρ' εὐθυδίκων
καλλίπαις πότμος ἀεί.

φιλεῖ δὲ τίκτειν ὕβρις μὲν παλαιὰ νεά-   στρ. δ'.
ζουσαν ἐν κακοῖς βροτῶν ὕβριν
τότ', ἢ τότ', εὖτ' ἂν τὸ κύριον μόλῃ.
†νεαρὰ φάους κότον
δαίμονά τε τὰν ἄμαχον, ἀπόλεμον,
ἀνίερον θράσος μελαί-
νας μελάθροισιν ἄτας,
εἰδομέναν τοκεῦσιν.

But soon she turned and made a bitter end
Of nuptial in old Ilion's hour of need—
　By Zeus, who punisheth when guests offend,
Sent thither as a bane to Priam's seed.
Kinship unblest !　Companionship unkind !
Sad bride of tears !　Fell fury unconfined !

Wise lips declared, and 'tis an agèd saw,
　That man's prosperity maturely grown
Hath offspring that succeeds by Heaven's high law,—
　From happy fortune misery full-blown.
A differing thought of mine shall be confessed :—

　The issue of impious deeds is impious still,
With plenteous increase, like to like succeeding ;
　Not so begets its race the righteous will,
But the fair life fair fortune aye is breeding.
No evil brood disturbs that peaceful nest.
The house of the upright evermore is blest.

The pride of former years engendereth pride
　Youngly insulting o'er calamity,—
Or soon or late, what matters ?—When the tide
　Of times brings on the hour of destiny
For that fell birth, even then is born the Power,
Unblest, resistless, making warriors cower,
　Infatuate Boldness, whose o'ershadowing gloom
　Veils all the house with darkness of the tomb.
Such parentage hath bloomed in such fell flower !

D

δίκα δὲ λάμπει μὲν ἐν δυσκάπνοις δώμασιν,   ἀντ. δ'.
τὸν δ' ἐναίσιμον τίει βίον.
τὰ χρυσόπαστ' ἐσθλὰ σὺν πίνῳ χερῶν
παλιντρόποις ὄμμασι λι-
ποῦσ', ὅσια προσέβα, τοῦ * *
δύναμιν οὐ σέβουσα πλού-
του παράσημον αἴνῳ·
πᾶν δ' ἐπὶ τέρμα νωμᾷ.

AGAMEMNON.

717—735.

ἔθρεψεν δὲ λέοντα   στρ. β'.
σίνιν δόμοις ἀγάλακτον
οὕτως ἀνὴρ φιλόμαστον,
ἐν βιότου προτελείοις
ἅμερον, εὐφιλόπαιδα,
καὶ γεραροῖς ἐπίχαρτον.
πολέα δ' ἔσχ' ἐν ἀγκάλαις,
νεοτρόφου τέκνου δίκαν,
φαιδρωπὸς ποτὶ χεῖρα, σαί-
νων τε γαστρὸς ἀνάγκαις.

χρονισθεὶς δ' ἀπέδειξεν   ἀντ. β'.
† ἔθος τὸ πρόσθε τοκήων.
χάριν τροφᾶς γὰρ ἀμείβων,
μηλοφόνοισιν ἄγαισιν
δαῖτ' ἀκέλευστυς ἔτευξεν·
αἵματι δ' οἶκος ἐφύρθη·
ἄμαχον ἄλγος οἰκέταις,
μέγα σίνος πολυκτόνον.
ἐκ θεοῦ δ' ἱερεύς τις ἄ-
τας δόμοις προσεθρέφθη.

The light of Righteousness in smoky homes
   Shines unimpaired, honouring the humble lot,
From gilded halls impure, as Earth she roams,
   She turns her gaze, to bless the pious cot ;
The power of riches, falsely stampt with praise,
Wins not her worship by its spurious blaze ;
   Her judgment ever points to the far goal
   Whereto she leads all lives with sure control,
Shaping the hour to suit with distant days.

LEWIS CAMPBELL.

AGAMEMNON.

717—735.

EVEN so, belike, might one
A lion suckling nurse,
Like a foster-son,
To his home a future curse.
In life's beginnings mild,
Dear to sire, and kind to child ;
Oft folded in his lord's embrace,
Like an infant of the race.
Sleek and smiling to the hand,
He fawned at want's command.

But in time he showed
The habit of his blood.
His debt of nurture he repaid ;
The lowing herds he tore,
A fierce unbidden feast he made,
And the house was foul with gore.
Huge grief its inmates overshed,
Huge mischief, slaughter widely spread !
A heaven-sent Priest of Woe
In the Palace did he grow.

W. E. GLADSTONE.

CHOEPHOROE.

20—83.

ἰαλτὸς ἐκ δόμων ἔβιιν   στρ. αʹ.
χοᾶν προπομπὸς ὀξύχειρι σὺν κτύπῳ.
πρέπει παρηὶς φοινίοις ἀμυγμοῖς
ὄνυχος ἄλοκι νεοτόμῳ·
δι᾽ αἰῶνος δ᾽ ἰυγμοῖσι βόσκεται κέαρ.
λινοφθόροι δ᾽ ὑφασμάτων
λακίδες ἔφλαδον ὑπ᾽ ἄλγεσιν,
πρόστερνοι στολμοὶ
πέπλων ἀγελάστοις
ξυμφοραῖς πεπληγμένων.

τορὸς γὰρ ὀρθόθριξ φόβος,   ἀντ. αʹ.
δόμων ὀνειρόμαντις, ἐξ ὕπνου κότον
πνέων, ἀωρόνυκτον ἀμβόαμα
μυχόθεν ἔλακε περὶ φόβῳ,
γυναικείοισιν ἐν δώμασιν βαρὺς πίτνων.
κριταί τε τῶνδ᾽ ὀνειράτων
θεόθεν ἔλακον ὑπέγγυοι
μέμφεσθαι τοὺς γᾶς
νέρθεν περιθύμως
τοῖς κτανοῦσί τ᾽ ἐγκοτεῖν.

CHOEPHORŒ.

20—83.

OBEDIENT to my Queen's command,
With pure libations in my hand,
  The regal halls I leave :
The shredded robe, the oft-dealt blow,
The bleeding cheek, whose furrows show
The handy-work of frantic woe,
   Bear witness how I grieve.
   Torn is the linen vest,
   That veiled my snowy breast ;
And smiles around my lips no longer play ;
   My heart, with care opprest,
Is fed on agony from day to day.
A cry the calm of midnight broke ;
From the dark chambers Terror spoke ;
Troubler of sleep !—with ghastly stare,
With breath of wrath, and bristling hair,
And accent shrill that pierced the ear,
Loud raved the dream-inspiring Seer !
Right heavily he sate, I ween,
Above the chambers of the Queen.
The interpreters, their troth who plight
   To spell the visions of the night,
   From God an answer gave :
" Sent forth by murdered man," they said,
" That form, to haunt the murderer's bed,
   Had issued from the grave."

τοιάνδε χάριν ἀχάριτον ἀπότρυπον κακῶν,   στρ. β'.
ἰὼ ϝαῖα μαῖα,
μωμένα μ' ἰάλλει
δύσθεος ϝυνά· φοβοῦ-
μαι δ' ἔπος τόδ' ἐκβαλεῖν.
τί ϝὰρ λύτρον πεσόντος αἵματος πέδοι;
ἰὼ πάνοιζυς ἑστία,
ἰὼ κατασκαφαὶ δόμων.
ἀνήλιοι, βροτοστυϝεῖς
δνόφοι καλύπτουσι δόμους
δεσποτῶν θανάτοισι.

σέβας δ' ἄμαχον, ἀδάματον, ἀπόλεμον τὸ πρὶν,   ἀντ. β'.
δι' ὤτων φρενός τε
δαμίας περαῖνον,
νῦν ἀφίσταται. φοβεῖ-
ται δέ τις. τὸ δ' εὐτυχεῖν
τόδ' ἐν βροτοῖς θεός τε καὶ θεοῦ πλέον.
ῥοπὰ δ' ἐπισκοπεῖ δίκας
ταχεῖα τοῖς μὲν ἐν φάει,
τὰ δ' ἐν μεταιχμίῳ σκότου
μένει χρονίζοντ' ἄχη βρύει·
τοὺς δ' ἄκρατος ἔχει νύξ.

δι' αἷματ' ἐκποθένθ' ὑπὸ χθονός τροφοῦ   στρ. ϝ'.
τίτας φόνος πέπηϝεν οὐ διαρρύδαν.
διαλϝὴς ἄτα διαφέρει τὸν αἴτιον

The impious Queen in vain these offerings sends,
To turn aside the ill that boding dream portends.
   Earth! her graceless gifts I pour thee!
   Earth, my mother! I adore thee:
   Yet scarce my tongue thy power may dare
   To mock with ineffectual prayer:
   Can aught remove the murderer's guilt?
   Can aught atone for life-blood spilt?
   Halls, o'erwhelmed in ruin rude!
   Hearth, where countless sorrows brood!
   Round you, now my Lord is slain,
   Sunless, hateful shadows reign;
   Loyal Faith that once possessed
   Every listening subject's breast,
   Faith, whose firmness seemed to mock
   War and foul sedition's shock,
   Hath past away;—the cravens bow
   Their necks beneath usurpers now.
   Man to success still court will pay,
   Still honour Fortune's fickle sway,
   Exalt her to the blest abodes,
   A Goddess and above the Gods.
   But Justice holds her equal scales
      With ever-waking eye;
   O'er some her vengeful might prevails,
      When their life's sun is high;
   On some her vigorous judgments light,
   In that dread pause twixt day and night,
      Life's closing twilight hour;
   Round some, ere yet they meet their doom,
   Is shed the silence of the tomb,
      The eternal shadows lower;
   But soon as once the genial plain
   Has drunk the life-blood of the slain,
   Indelible the spots remain,

παναρκέτας νόσου.

οἴγοντι δ' οὔτι νυμφικῶν ἑδωλίων   ἀντ. ϛ΄.
ἄκος, πόροι τε πάντες ἐκ μιᾶς ὁδοῦ
βαίνοντες τὸν χερομυσῆ
φόνον καθαίροντες ἰοῦσαν ἄτην.

ἐμοὶ δ', ἀνάγκαν γὰρ ἀμφίπτολιν
θεοὶ προσήνεγκιν. ἐκ γὰρ οἴκων
πατρῴων δούλιον ἐσᾶγον αἶσαν,
δίκαια καὶ μὴ δίκαια,
πρέποντ' ἀρχαῖς βίου,
βίᾳ φερομένων αἰνέσαι, πικρὸν φρενῶν
στύγος κρατούσῃ. δακρύω δ' ὑφ' εἱμάτων
ματαίοισι δεσποτᾶν
τύχαις, κρυφαίοις πένθεσιν παχνουμένη.

And aye for vengeance call,
Till racking pangs of piercing pain
    Upon the guilty fall.
What balm for him shall potent prove,
Who breaks the ties of wedded love?
And though all streams united gave
The treasures of their limpid wave,
    To purify from gore ;
The hand, polluted once with blood,
Though washed in every silver flood,
    Is foul for evermore !
Hard Fate is mine, since that dark day,
Which girt my home with war's array,
And bore me from my father's hall,
To pine afar, a captive thrall ;
Hard Fate ! to yield to Heaven's decree,
And what I am not, seem to be ;
Dissemble hatred, and control
The bitter workings of the soul ;
E'en to injustice feign consent ;
Detest the wrong, but not prevent :
Yet oft I veil my face, to weep
For those who unavengèd sleep ;
Oft for my slaughtered lord I mourn,
Chilled by the frost of grief, with secret anguish torn !

JOSEPH ANSTICE.

EUMENIDES.

307—396.

ἄγε δὴ καὶ χορὸν ἄψωμεν, ἐπεὶ
μοῦσαν στυγερὰν
ἀποφαίνεσθαι δεδόκηκε,
λέξαι τε λάχη τὰ κατ' ἀνθρώπους
ὡς ἐπινωμᾷ στάσις ἅμα,
εὐθυδίκαι θ' ἡδόμεθ' εἶναι.
τὸν μὲν καθαρὰς χεῖρας προνέμοντ'
οὔτις ἀφ' ἡμῶν μῆνις ἐφέρπει,
ἀσινὴς δ' αἰῶνα διοιχνεῖ·
ὅστις δ' ἀλιτὼν ὥσπερ ὅδ' ἀνὴρ
χεῖρας φονίας ἐπικρύπτει,
μάρτυρες ὀρθαὶ τοῖσι θανοῦσιν
παραγιγνόμεναι πράκτορες αἵματος
αὐτῷ τελέως ἐφάνημεν.

μᾶτερ, ἅ μ' ἔτικτες, ὦ μᾶτερ   στρ. α'.
Νὺξ ἀλαοῖσι καὶ δεδορκόσιν
ποινάν, κλῦθ'. ὁ Λατοῦς γὰρ ἶ-
νίς μ' ἄτιμον τίθησι,
τόνδ' ἀφαιρούμενος
πτῶκα, ματρῷον ἅ-
γνισμα κύριον φόνου.
ἐπὶ δὲ τῷ τεθυμένῳ
τόδε μέλος, παρακοπά,
παραφορὰ φρενοδαλὴς,
ὕμνος ἐξ Ἐρινύων,
δέσμιος φρενῶν, ἀφόρ-
μικτος, αὐονὰ βροτοῖς.

EUMENIDES.

307—396.

Up and lead the dance of Fate!
Lift the song that mortals hate!
Tell what rights are ours on earth,
Over all of human birth.
Swift of foot t' avenge are we!
   He whose hands are clean and pure,
Nought our wrath to dread hath he;
   Calm his cloudless days endure.

But the man that seeks to hide,
   Like him, his gore-bedewèd hands,
Witnesses to them that died,
The blood avengers at his side,
   The Furies' troop for ever stands.

Mother! that us thy sacred brood did'st bear!
     O mother Night!
Us, owned by all—the blind to earthly light,
And those that yet behold Heaven's sunshine bright,
  The Powers of vengeance, hear!
  See us dishonoured by Latona's son,
      Who far hath rent away
      This our devoted prey,
For deed of murder on his mother done.
    O'er our victim come begin!
     Come, the incantation sing,
     Frantic all and maddening,
   To the heart a brand of fire,
      The Furies' hymn,
    That which chains the senses dim,
   Tuneless to the gentle lyre,
     Withering the soul within.

τοῦτο γὰρ λάχος διανταία   ἀντ. α΄.
μοῖρ᾽ ἐπέκλωσεν ἐμπέδως
ἔχειν, θνατῶν τοῖσιν αὐτουργίαι
ξυμπέσωσιν μάταιοι,
τοῖς ὁμαρτεῖν, ὄφρ᾽ ἂν
γᾶν ὑπέλθῃ· θανὼν δ᾽
οὐκ ἄγαν ἐλεύθερος.
ἐπὶ δὲ τῷ τεθυμένῳ
τόδε μέλος, παρακοπά,
παραφορὰ φρενοδαλής,
ὕμνος ἐξ Ἐρινύων,
δέσμιος φρενῶν, ἀφόρ-
μικτος, αὐονὰ βροτοῖς.

γιγνομέναισι λάχη   στρ. β΄.
τάδ᾽ ἐφ᾽ ἁμὶν ἐκράνθη·
ἀθανάτων δ᾽ ἀπέχειν
χέρας, οὐδέ τις ἐστὶ
συνδαίτωρ μετάκοινος.
παλλεύκων δὲ πέπλων
ἄμοιρος, ἄκληρος ἐτύχθην.
ζωμάτων γὰρ εἱλόμαν
ἀνατροπάς, ὅταν Ἄρης
τιθασὸς ὢν φίλον ἕλῃ·
†ἐπὶ τὸν, ὦ, διόμεναι
κρατερὸν ὄνθ᾽, ὁμοίως
μαυροῦμεν ὑφ᾽ αἵματος νέου.

σπευδόμεναι δ᾽ ἀφελεῖν   ἀντ. β΄.
τινὰ τάσδε μερίμνας,
θεῶν δ᾽ ἀτέλειαν ἐμαῖ-
σι λιταῖς ἐπικραίνειν,

Even at our birth the Fates decreed
To us the everlasting meed ;
Whoe'er untimely blood hath spilt,
Loading his soul with murtherous guilt ;
   His restless followers still to be,
Even till he refuge take beneath
The darksome earth, nor yet in death
     From our inevitable presence free.
      O'er our victim come begin !
        Come, the incantation sing,
        Frantic all and maddening,
      To the heart a brand of fire,
         The Furies' hymn,
        That which chains the senses dim,
      Tuneless to the gentle lyre,
        Withering the soul within.

Such at our birth our lot was given,
Ne'er to approach the immortal Gods of heaven,
   Nor ever at the joyous feast
   Was deity of light our guest,
Nor share nor portion e'er had we
In the white robes of their festivity.
   We the task of ruin chose,
   T' o'erthrow the palaces of those
   Who in the bloody civil strife
   Stain their hands with kindred life.
   Him our restless feet pursue ;
     In his triumphant hour,
   And while the reeking blood is new,
     We crush him in his power.

   We thus the weight of care remove
   From the great avenging Jove.
Thus men of blood our imprecations free
From judgment of each other deity ;

μηδ' εἰς ἄˠκρισιν ἐλθεῖν.
Ζεὺς ˠὰρ αἱματοσταˠὲς
ἀξιόμισον ἔθνος τόδε λέσχας
ἃς ἀπηξιώσατο.
† μάλα ˠὰρ οὖν ἁλομένα
ἄˠκαθεν βαρυπεσῆ
καταφέρω ποδὸς ἀκμὰν,
σφαλερὰ τανυδρόμοις
κῶλα, δύσφορον ἄταν.†

† δόξαι τ' ἀνδρῶν καὶ μάλ' ὑπ' αἰθέρι σεμναὶ   στρ. ˠ'.
τακόμεναι κατὰ ˠᾶν μινύθουσιν ἄτιμοι
ἁμετέραις ἐφόδοις μελανείμοσιν ὀρχησμοῖς τ' ἐπιφθόνοις
ποδός.†

πίπτων δ' οὐκ οἶδεν τόδ' ὑπ' ἄφρονι λύμα.   ἀντ. ˠ'.
τοῖον ἐπὶ κνέφας ἀνδρὶ μύσος πεπόταται,
καὶ δνοφερὰν τιν' ἀχλὺν κατὰ δώματος αὐδᾶται πολύστονος
φάτις.

μένει ˠάρ· εὐμήχανοι   στρ. δ'.
δὲ καὶ τέλειοι, κακῶν
τε μνήμονες σεμναὶ,
καὶ δυσπαρήˠοροι βροτοῖς,
ἄτιμ' ἀτίετα διόμεναι
λάχη θεῶν διχοστατοῦντ'
ἀναλίῳ λάπᾳ, δυσοδοπαίπαλα
δερκομένοισι καὶ δυσομμάτοις ὁμῶς.

τίς οὖν τάδ' οὐχ ἄζεται   ἀντ. δ'.
τε καὶ δέδοικεν βροτῶν,
ἐμοῦ κλύων θεσμὸν
τὸν μοιρόκραντον ἐκ θεῶν
δοθέντα τέλεον; ἐπὶ δέ μοι
ˠέρας παλαιὸν, οὐδ'
ἀτιμίας κυρῶ, καίπερ ὑπὸ χθόνα
τάξιν ἔχουσα καὶ δυσάλιον κνέφας.

For highest Jove this hateful race
Forbids to stand before his awful face.
   The pride of all of human birth,
     All glorious in the eye of day,
     Dishonoured slowly melts away,
   Trod down and trampled to the earth,
   Whene'er our dark-stoled troop advances,
   Whene'er our feet lead on the dismal dances.

   For leaping down from high, I place
My stern foot's ponderous weight,
   Supplanting him in his triumphant race,
And hurling him down headlong—awful fate !
He whom the darkness of his guilt o'erclouds
   In sin's blind dulness still the doom defies,
Till through the gloom his fated house that shrouds,
   Wail feebly forth the many-voicèd cries.

   For light our footsteps are,
     And perfect is our might,
Awful remembrancers of guilt and crime,
   Implacable to mortal prayer,
Far from the gods, unhonoured, and heaven's light,
   We hold our voiceless dwellings dread,
All unapproached by living or by dead.

   What mortal feels not awe,
Nor trembles at our name,
Hearing our fate-appointed power sublime,
   Fixed by the eternal law ?
For old our office, and our fame,
   Might never yet of its due honours fail,
Though 'neath the earth our realm in unsunn'd regions
     pale.

               DEAN MILMAN.

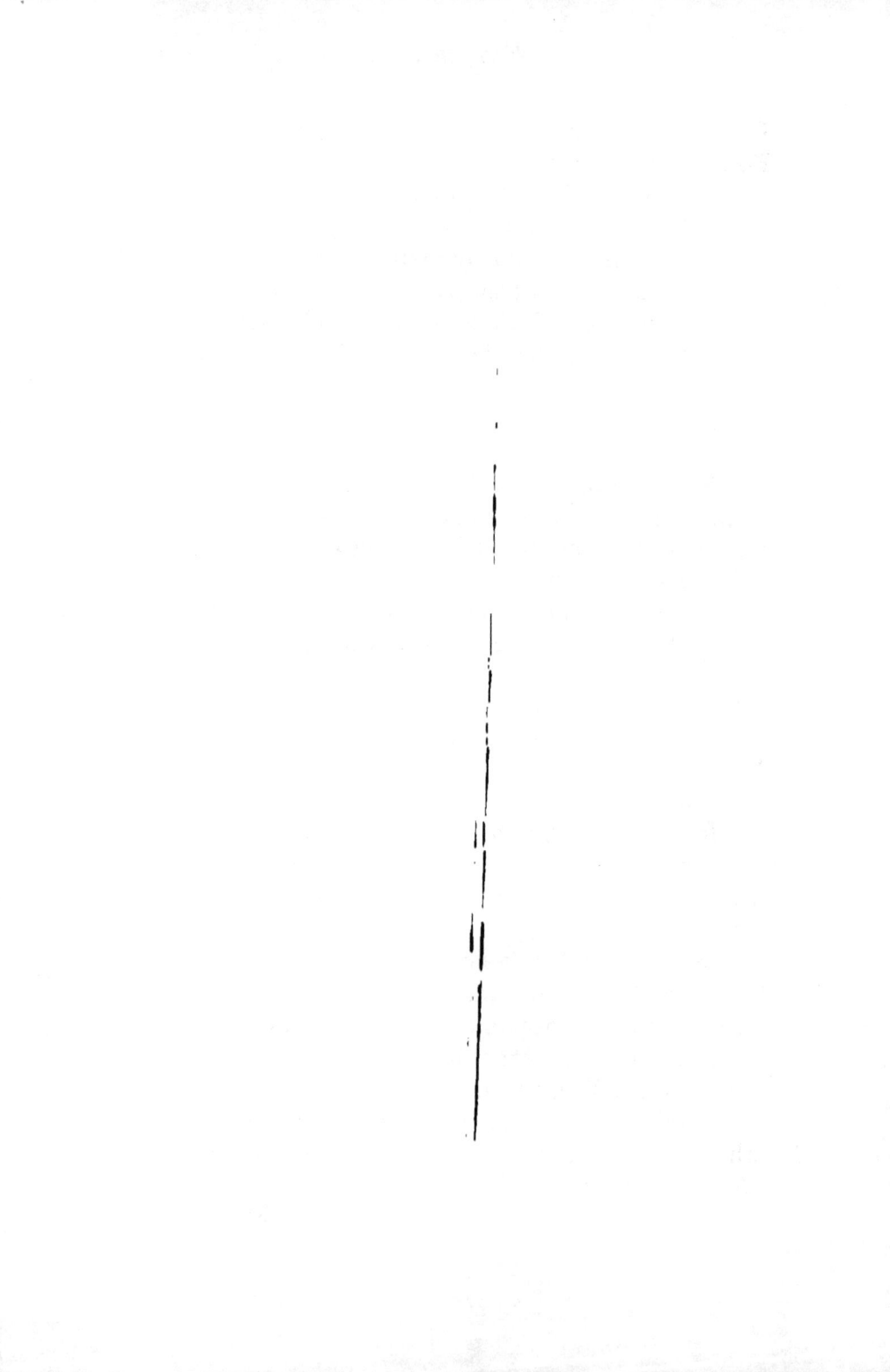

SOPHOCLES.

E

AJAX.

596—645.

ὦ κλεινὰ Σαλαμίς, σὺ μέν που   στρ. α'.
ναίεις ἁλίπλακτος, εὐδαίμων,
πᾶσιν περίφαντος ἀεί·
ἐγὼ δ' ὁ τλάμων παλαιὸς ἀφ' οὗ χρόνος
Ἰδαῖα μίμνω λειμῶνι' ἄποινα, μηνῶν
ἀνήριθμος αἰὲν εὐνώμα
χρόνῳ τρυχόμενος,
κακὰν ἐλπίδ' ἔχων
ἔτι μέ ποτ' ἀνύσειν
τὸν ἀπότροπον ἀΐζηλον Ἅιδαν.

καί μοι δυσθεράπευτος Αἴας   ἀντ. α'.
ξύνεστιν ἔφεδρος, ὤμοι μοι,
θείᾳ μανίᾳ ξύναυλος·
ὃν ἐξεπέμψω πρὶν δή ποτε θουρίῳ
κρατοῦντ' ἐν Ἄρει· νῦν δ' αὖ φρενὸς οἰοβώτας
φίλοις μέγα πένθος ηὕρηται.
τὰ πρὶν δ' ἔργα χεροῖν
μεγίστας ἀρετᾶς
ἄφιλα παρ' ἀφίλοις
ἔπεσ' ἔπεσε μελέοις Ἀτρείδαις.

ἦ που παλαιᾷ μὲν ἔντροφος ἀμέρᾳ,   στρ. β'.
λευκῷ δὲ γήρᾳ μάτηρ νιν ὅταν νοσοῦντα
φρενομόρως ἀκούσῃ,
αἴλινον αἴλινον
οὐδ' οἰκτρᾶς γόον ὄρνιθος ἀηδοῦς
ἥσει δύσμορος, ἀλλ' ὀξυτόνους μὲν ᾠδὰς
θρηνήσει, χερόπληκτοι δ'
ἐν στέρνοισι πεσοῦνται
δοῦποι καὶ πολιᾶς ἄμυγμα χαίτας.

AJAX.

596—645.

FAIR Salamis, the billow's roar
    Wanders around thee yet ;
And sailors gaze upon thy shore
    Firm in the Ocean set.
Thy son is in a foreign clime
    Where Ida feeds her countless flocks,
    Far from thy dear remembered rocks,
Worn by the waste of time,—
Comfortless, nameless, hopeless,—save
In the dark prospect of the yawning grave.

And Ajax, in his deep distress
    Allied to our disgrace,
Hath cherished in his loneliness
    The bosom friend's embrace.
Frenzy hath seized thy dearest son,
    Who from thy shores in glory came
    The first in valour and in fame ;
The deeds that he hath done
Seem hostile all to hostile eyes ;
The sons of Atreus see them and despise.

Woe to the mother, in her close of day,
Woe to her desolate heart, and temples gray,
    When she shall hear
Her loved one's story whispered in her ear !
    "Woe, woe !" will be the cry,—
No quiet murmur like the tremulous wail
Of the lone bird, the querulous nightingale,—
    But shrieks that fly
Piercing, and wild, and loud, shall mourn the tale ;
And she will beat her breast, and rend her hair,
Scattering the silver locks that Time hath left her there.

E 2

κρείσσων παρ' Ἅιδᾳ κεύθων ὁ νοσῶν μάταν,   ἀντ. β΄.
ὃς ἐκ πατρῴας ἥκων γενεᾶς ἄριστος
πολυπόνων Ἀχαιῶν,
οὐκ ἔτι συντρόφοις
ὀργαῖς ἔμπεδος, ἀλλ' ἐκτὸς ὁμιλεῖ.
ὦ τλᾶμον πάτερ, οἵαν σε μένει πυθέσθαι
παιδὸς δύσφορον ἄταν,
ἃν οὔπω τις ἔθρεψεν
αἰὼν Αἰακιδᾶν ἄτερθε τοῦδε.

AJAX.

693—718.

ἔφριξ' ἔρωτι, περιχαρὴς δ' ἀνεπτόμαν.   στρ.
ἰὼ ἰὼ Πὰν Πάν,
ὦ Πὰν Πὰν ἁλίπλαγκτε, Κυλλανίας χιονοκτύπου
πετραίας ἀπὸ δειράδος φάνηθ', ὦ
θεῶν χοροποί' ἄναξ, ὅπως μοι
Νύσια Κνώσι' ὀρχήματ' αὐτοδαῆ
ξυνὼν ἰάψῃς.
νῦν γὰρ ἐμοὶ μέλει χορεῦσαι.
Ἰκαρίων δ' ὑπὲρ πελαγέων μολὼν ἄναξ Ἀπόλλων
ὁ Δάλιος εὔγνωστος
ἐμοὶ ξυνείη διὰ παντὸς εὔφρων.

Oh ! when the pride of Græcia's noblest race
Wanders, as now, in darkness and disgrace,
   When Reason's day
Sets rayless—joyless—quenched in cold decay,
   Better to die, and sleep
The never-waking sleep, than linger on,
And dare to live, when the soul's life is gone :
   But thou shalt weep,
Thou wretched father, for thy dearest son,
Thy best beloved, by inward Furies torn,
The deepest, bitterest curse, thine ancient house hath
  borne !
     WINTHROP MACKWORTH PRAED.

AJAX.

693—718.

A SHUDDER of love thrills through me. Joy ! I soar !
  O Pan, wild Pan !   [*They dance.*]
  Come from Cyllene hoar—
Come from the snow-drift, the rock-ridge, the glen !
  Leaving the mountain bare
  Fleet through the salt sea-air,
Mover of dances to Gods and to men.
Whirl me in Cnossian ways—thrid me the Nysian maze !
Come, while the joy of the dance is my care !
  Thou too, Apollo, come,
  Bright from thy Delian home,
   Bringer of day,
  Fly o'er the southward main
  Here in our hearts to reign,
Loved to repose there and kindly to stay.

ἔλυ϶εν αἰνὸν ἄχος ἀπ' ὀμμάτων Ἄρης.   ἀντ.
ἰὼ ἰώ. νῦν αὖ,
νῦν, ὦ Ζεῦ, πάρα λευκὸν εὐάμερον πελάσαι φάος
θοᾶν ὠκυάλων νεῶν, ὅτ' Αἴας
λαθίπονος πάλιν, θεῶν δ' αὖ
πάνθυτα θέ϶μι' ἐξήνυ϶' εὐνομίᾳ
σέβων μεγί϶τᾳ.
πάνθ' ὁ μέγας χρόνος μαραίνει,
κοὐδὲν ἀναύδατον φατίϲαιμ' ἂν, εὖτέ ϝ' ἐξ ἀέλπτων
Αἴας μετανεγνώϲθη
θυμοῦ τ' Ἀτρείδαις μεγάλων τε νεικέων.

ŒDIPUS TYRANNUS.

151—215.

ὦ Διὸς ἀδυεπὲς φάτι,   ϲτρ. α'.
τίς ποτε τᾶς πολυχρύϲου
Πυθῶνος ἀγλαὰς ἔβας
Θήβας; ἐκτέταμαι φοβε-
ρὰν φρένα, δείματι πάλλων,
ἰήιε Δάλιε Παιαν,
ἀμφὶ ϲοὶ ἁ϶όμενος, τί μοι ἢ νέον,
ἢ περιτελλομέναις ὥραις πάλιν
ἐξανύϲεις χρέος. εἰπέ μοι, ὦ χρυϲέ-
ας τέκνον Ἐλπίδος, ἄμβροτε Φάμα.

Horror is past.   Our eyes have rest from pain.
  O Lord of Heaven !   [*They dance.*]
  Now blithesome day again
Purely may smile on our swift-sailing fleet,
  Since, all his woe forgot,
  Aias now faileth not
Aught that of prayer and Heaven-worship is meet.
Time bringeth mighty aid—nought but in time doth fade :
Nothing shall move me as strange to my thought.
  Aias, our lord, hath now
  Cleared his wrath-burdened brow
   Long our despair,
  Ceased from his angry feud
  And with mild heart renewed
Peace and goodwill to the high-sceptred pair.

        LEWIS CAMPBELL.

ŒDIPUS TYRANNUS.

151—215.

LORD of the Pythian treasure,
  What meaneth the word thou hast spoken ?
  The strange and wondrous word,
   Which Thebes hath heard,
Oh ! it hath shaken our hearts to a faltering measure !
  A token, O Paian, a token !
  What is thy boon to us ?
  Shall it come soon to us,
  Shall it be long e'er the circle bend
  Full round to the fatal end ?
Answer us, daughter of Hope,
  Voice born Immortal of golden Hope !

πρῶτά σε κεκλόμενος, θύγα-   ἀντ. α΄.
τερ Διος, ἄμβροτ᾽ Ἀθάνα,
γαιάοχύν τ᾽ ἀδελφεὰν
Ἄρτεμιν, ἃ κυκλόεντ᾽ ἀγο-
ρᾶς θρόνον εὐκλέα θάσσει,
καὶ Φοῖβον ἑκαβόλον, ἰὼ
τρισσοὶ ἀλεξίμοροι προφάνητέ μοι,
εἴ ποτε καὶ προτέρας ἄτας ὑπερ-
ορνυμένας πόλει ἠνύσατ᾽ ἐκτοπί-
αν φλόγα πήματος, ἔλθετε καὶ νῦν.

ὦ πόποι, ἀνάριθμα γὰρ φέρω   στρ. β΄.
πήματα· νοσεῖ δέ μοι πρόπας
στόλος, οὐδ᾽ ἔνι φροντίδος ἔγχος
ᾧ τις ἀλέξεται. οὔτε γὰρ ἔκγονα
κλυτᾶς χθονὸς αὔξεται οὔτε τόκοισιν
ἰηίων καμάτων ἀνέ-
χουσι γυναῖκες·
ἄλλον δ᾽ ἂν ἄλλῳ προσί-
δοις ἅπερ εὔπτερον ὄρνιν
κρεῖσσον ἀμαιμακέτου πυρὸς ὄρμενον
ἀκτὰν πρὸς ἑσπέρου θεοῦ·

ὧν πόλις ἀνάριθμος ὄλλυται·   ἀντ. β΄.
νηλέα δὲ γένεθλα πρὸς πέδῳ
θαναταφόρα κεῖται ἀνοίκτως·
ἐν δ᾽ ἄλοχοι πολιαί τ᾽ ἔπι ματέρες
ἀκτὰν παρὰ βώμιον ἄλλοθεν ἄλλαι
λυγρῶν πόνων ἱκτῆρες ἐ-
πιστενάχουσιν.
παιὰν δὲ λάμπει στονό-
εσσά τε γῆρυς ὅμαυλος·
ὧν ὕπερ, ὦ χρυσέα θύγατερ Διὸς,
εὐῶπα πέμψον ἀλκάν·

First therefore thou be entreated,
      Divine unapproachable maiden,
And Artemis with thee, our aid to be,
In the mid mart of our city majestical seated,
     And Phœbus the archer death-laden!
     By your affinity
     Helpfullest trinity,
Help us. And as in the time gone by
     Ye have bowed to our plaintive cry,
Bowed to our misery sore :
     So come to us now as ye came before.

Ah me! it is a world, a world of woe,
Plague upon the height and plague below !
     And they mow us with murderous glaive,
     And never a shield to save !
Never a fruit of the earth comes to the birth,
     And in vain, in vain
Is the cry and the labour of mothers, and all for a fruit-
     Away, away,   [less pain.
Ghost upon ghost they are wafted away :
     One with another they die,
     Swifter than flame do they fly
     From life, from light, from day.

Ah me ! it is a world, a world of dead,
Feverous and foul, with corpses spread :
     And they lie as they lie, unbefriended.
Where are the mothers, and where are the wives?
     They are fled, fled for their lives,
     To the altars to pray,
     There to lie, to sigh,
And to pray, and to pray unattended,
     With choir and cry
Lamentation and litany blended.
And only, O Maiden, by thee may our marred estate be
   mended.

Ἀρεά τε τὸν μαλερὸν, ὃς   στρ. ʹ.
νῦν ἄχαλκος ἀσπίδων
φλέγει με περιβόητος ἀντιάζων,
παλίσσυτον δρόμημα νωτίσαι πάτρας
†ἄπουρον, εἴτ᾽ ἐς μέγαν
θάλαμον Ἀμφιτρίτας
εἴτ᾽ ἐς τὸν ἀπόξενον ὅρμον
Θρήκιον κλύδωνα·
†τέλει ʹάρ εἴ τι νὺξ ἀφῇ,
τοῦτ᾽ ἐπ᾽ ἦμαρ ἔρχεται·
τὸν, ὦ τᾶν πυρφόρων
ἀστραπᾶν κράτη νέμων,
ὦ Ζεῦ πάτερ, ὑπὸ σῷ φθίσον κεραυνῷ.

Λύκει᾽ ἄναξ, τά τε σα χρυ-   ἀντ. ʹ.
σοστρόφων ἀπ᾽ ἀʹκυλᾶν
βέλεα θέλοιμ᾽ ἂν ἀδάματ᾽ ἐνδατεῖσθαι
†ἀρωʹὰ προσταχθέντα, τάς τε πυρφόρους
Ἀρτέμιδος αἴʹλας, ἐὺν αἷς
Λύκι᾽ ὅρεα διάσσει·
τὸν χρυσομίτραν τε κικλήσκω,
τᾶσδ᾽ ἐπώνυμον ʹᾶς,
οἰνῶπα Βάκχον εὔιον,
Μαινάδων ὁμόστολον,
πελασθῆναι φλέʹοντ᾽
ἀʹλαῶπι * * *
πεύκᾳ ᾽πὶ τὸν ἀπότιμον ἐν θεοῖς θεόν.

The fiend of plague, whose swordless hand
Burns like battle through the land,
With wild tempestuous wailing all about him,—
O cross his track and turn him back
O meet him, thou, and rout him!
Let him sink again
Deep in the deepest main!
Let him mingle in horrible motion
With the wildest ocean!
(For still what scapes the cruel night,
Cruel day destroys it quite.)
But oh! with thunder-stroke
Let our enemy and thine be broke,—
O Zeus!—
Father!—let him know thy wrath, thy wrath divine!

O God of light, from lightsome bow
Cast abroad thy fiery snow,
Like morsels cast thine arrowy, fiery snow!
And thou, O mountain maiden pure,
His sister, stand our champion sure,
Stand and strow
Arrows, as fire, below!
Thou too—thou art Theban—O Bacchus,
Thou—art thou not Theban?—O Bacchus,
In rosy bloom, elate and strong,
Lead thy madding train along,
Until thy fiery chase
Hunt the demon from the place
Afar, afar!
O follow, follow him far, afar!

A. W. VERRALL.

OEDIPUS TYRANNUS.

863—910.

εἴ μοι ξυνείη φέροντι   στρ. α΄.
μοῖρα τὰν εὔσεπτον ἁγνείαν λόγων
ἔργων τε πάντων, ὧν νόμοι πρόκεινται
ὑψίποδες, οὐρανίαν
δι᾿ αἰθέρα τεκνωθέντες, ὧν Ὄλυμπος
πατὴρ μόνος, οὐδέ νιν
θνατὰ φύσις ἀνέρων
ἔτικτεν, οὐδὲ μήν ποτε λάθα κατακοιμάσει·
μέγας ἐν τούτοις θεός, οὐδὲ γηράσκει.

ὕβρις φυτεύει τύραννον·   ἀντ. α΄.
ὕβρις, εἰ πολλῶν ὑπερπλησθῇ μάταν,
ἃ μὴ ᾿πίκαιρα μηδὲ συμφέροντα,
ἀκρότατον εἰσαναβᾶσ᾿
* * ἀπότομον ὤρουσεν εἰς ἀνάγκαν,   .
ἔνθ᾿ οὐ ποδὶ χρησίμῳ
χρῆται. τὸ καλῶς δ᾿ ἔχον
πόλει πάλαισμα μήποτε λῦσαι θεὸν αἰτοῦμαι.
θεὸν οὐ λήξω ποτὲ προστάταν ἴσχων.

εἰ δέ τις ὑπέροπτα χερσὶν   στρ. β΄.
ἢ λόγῳ πορεύεται,
Δίκας ἀφόβητος, οὐδὲ
δαιμόνων ἕδη σέβων,
κακά νιν ἕλοιτο μοῖρα,
δυσπότμου χάριν χλιδᾶς,
εἰ μὴ τὸ κέρδος κερδανεῖ δικαίως
καὶ τῶν ἀσέπτων ἔρξεται,
ἢ τῶν ἀθίκτων ἕξεται ματάζων.
τίς ἔτι ποτ᾿ ἐν τοῖσδ᾿ ἀνὴρ θυμοῦ βέλη
εὔξεται ψυχᾶς ἀμύνειν;

ŒDIPUS TYRANNUS.

863—910.

MINE be it, mine to hold,
With destiny to aid, the stainless sanctity
    In words and actions manifold,
Whereof the laws do live and move on high,
    Set in eternal spheres,
Born in the bright expanse of upper sky,
Birth of the high God, not of mortal years,
    Nor unto dull oblivion a prey :
Strong, ageless deity is theirs, and waneth not away.

    The child of earthly pride
Is tyranny, when once man's life doth teem
With wealth too great to profit or beseem.
    Up, by a path untried,
Up to the crowning peak of bliss
She climbs, then headlong down the sheer abyss
    Helpless she sinks to the unfooted void !
Yet unto God I pray that he may ne'er annul
Man's strife that man's estate be honoured to the full.
God is my help ; to him my faith clings undestroyed.

    But if a man, in deed or word,
    Walks o'er-informed with pride and might,
    By fear of justice undeterred,
    Scorning the seats of deity,
    Ill doom, to that man drawing nigh,
    His ill-starred arrogance requite !
    Unless toward his proper gain
    With uncorrupted hand he strain,
    Unless he loathe all filthiness—
If with lewd hands he touch the grace of holiness !
Henceforth, if such things be, no mortal evermore
        Can from his life repel
The darts of heaven and boast that foiled they fell :

εἰ γὰρ αἱ τοιαίδε πράξεις τίμιαι,
τί δεῖ με χορεύειν;

οὐκ ἔτι τὸν ἄθικτον εἶμι   ἀντ. β′.
γᾶς ἐπ' ὀμφαλὸν σέβων,
οὐδ' ἐς τὸν Ἄβαισι ναὸν,
οὐδὲ τὰν Ὀλυμπίαν,
εἰ μὴ τάδε χειρύδεικτα
πᾶσιν ἁρμόσει βροτοῖς.
ἀλλ', ὦ κρατύνων, εἴπερ ὄρθ' ἀκούεις,
Ζεῦ πάντ' ἀνάσσων, μὴ λάθοι
σὲ τάν τε σὰν ἀθάνατον αἰὲν ἀρχάν.
φθίνοντα γὰρ * * * Λαΐυυ
θέσφατ' ἐξαιροῦσιν ἤδη,
κοὐδαμοῦ τιμαῖς Ἀπόλλων ἐμφανής·
ἔρρει δὲ τὰ θεῖα.

ŒDIPUS COLONEUS.
668—719.

εὐίππου, ξένε, τᾶσδε χώρας   στρ. α′.
ἵκου τὰ κράτιστα γᾶς ἔπαυλα,
τὸν ἀργῆτα Κολωνὸν, ἔνθ'
ἁ λίγεια μινύρεται
θαμίζουσα μάλιστ' ἀηδὼν
χλωραῖς ὑπὸ βάσσαις,
τὸν οἰνῶπα νέμουσα κισσὸν

If he who walks such ways
Deserve man's honour and his praise,
Wherefore with holy dance should I the Gods adore?

Never again from Delphi's central hearth,
 The sacred spot inviolate of earth,
  Will I seek Phœbus' grace,
  Nor unto Abae nor Olympia go,
Unless these presages come forth,
Clear, to the issue joined, for all to see and show.
 But unto thee we pray,
Zeus, lord and king! if so men call on thee aright—
 Deathless thou art, eternal, full of sway—
 Let not transgression 'scape thy sight!
  Wrecks of a bygone day,
The ancient oracles of Laius' line
Are cast contemned away!
No more is glorified Apollo's shrine;
 Death falls on things divine.

E. D. A. MORSHEAD.

ŒDIPUS COLONEUS.

668—719.

STRANGER, thou art standing now
On Colonos' sparry brow;
All the haunts of Attic ground,
Where the matchless coursers bound,
Boast not, through their realms of bliss,
Other spot as fair as this.
Frequent down this greenwood dale,
Mourns the warbling nightingale,
Nestling mid the thickest screen
Of the ivy's darksome green;

καὶ τὰν ἄβατον θεοῦ
φυλλάδα μυριόκαρπον ἀνήλιον
ἀνήνεμόν τε πάντων
χειμώνων· ἵν' ὁ βακχιώτας
ἀεὶ Διόνυσος ἐμβατεύει
θεαῖς ἀμφιπολῶν τιθήναις.

θάλλει δ' οὐρανίας ὑπ' ἄχνας   ἀντ. α'.
ὁ καλλίβοτρυς κατ' ἦμαρ ἀεὶ
νάρκισσος, μεγάλαιν θεαῖν
ἀρχαῖον στεφάνωμ', ὅ τε
χρυσαυγὴς κρόκος· οὐδ' ἄϋπνοι
κρῆναι μινύθουσιν
Κηφισοῦ νομάδες ῥεέθρων,
ἀλλ' αἰὲν ἐπ' ἦματι
ὠκυτόκος πεδίων ἐπινίσσεται
ἀκηράτῳ ξὺν ὄμβρῳ
στερνούχου χθονός· οὐδὲ Μουσᾶν
χοροί νιν ἀπεστύγησαν, οὐδ' ἁ
χρυσάνιος Ἀφροδίτα.

ἔστιν δ' οἷον ἐγὼ γᾶς Ἀσίας οὐκ ἐπακούω,   στρ. β'.
οὐδ' ἐν τᾷ μεγάλᾳ   .
Δωρίδι νάσῳ Πέλοπος
πώποτε βλαστὸν
φύτευμ' ἀχείρητον αὐτόποιον,

Or where, each empurpled shoot
Drooping with its myriad fruit,
Curled in many a mazy twine,
Blooms the never-trodden vine,
By the God's protecting power
Safe from sun and storm and shower.
Bacchus here, the summer long,
Revels with the Goddess throng,
Nymphs who erst, on Nyssa's wild,
Reared to man the rosy child.

　Here Narcissus, day by day,
Buds, in clustering beauty gay,
Sipping aye, at morn and even,
All the nectar dews of heaven,
Wont amid your locks to shine,
Ceres fair, and Proserpine.
Here the golden Crocus gleams,
Murmur here unfailing streams,
Sleep the bubbling fountains never,
Feeding pure Cephisus river,
Whose prolific waters daily
Bid the pastures blossom gaily,
With the showers of spring-tide blending,
On the lap of earth descending.
Here the Nine, to notes of pleasure,
Love to tread their choral measure,
Venus, o'er those flow'rets gliding,
Oft her rein of gold is guiding.

　Now a brighter boast than all
Shall my grateful song recall ;
Yon proud shrub, that will not smile,
Pelops, on thy Doric isle,
Nor on Asiatic soil,
But unsown, unsought by toil,
Self-engendered, year by year,

ἐγχέων φόβημα δαΐων,
ὃ τᾷδε θάλλει μέγιστα χώρᾳ,
γλαυκᾶς παιδοτρόφου φύλλον ἐλαίας·
τὸ μέν τις οὔθ’ ἱβὸς οὔτε γήρᾳ
σημαίνων ἁλιώσει χερὶ πέρ-
σας· ὁ γὰρ αἰὲν ὁρῶν κύκλος
λεύσσει νιν Μορίου Διὸς
χἁ γλαυκῶπις Ἀθάνα.

ἄλλον δ’ αἶνον ἔχω ματροπόλει τᾷδε κράτιστον,   ἀντ. β’.
ἑῶρον τοῦ μεγάλου
δαίμονος, εἰπεῖν, χθονὸς αὔ-
χημα μέγιστον,
εὔιππον, εὔπωλον, εὐθάλασσον.
ὦ παῖ Κρόνου, σὺ γάρ νιν ἐς
τόδ’ εἶσας αὔχημ’, ἄναξ Ποσειδάν,
ἵπποισιν τὸν ἀκεστῆρα χαλινὸν
πρώταισι ταῖσδε κτίσας ἀγυιαῖς.
ἁ δ’ εὐήρετμος ἔκπαγλ’ ἁλία
χερσὶ παραπτομένα πλάτα
θρώσκει, τῶν ἑκατομπόδων
Νηρῄδων ἀκόλουθος.

Springs to life a native here.
Tree the trembling foeman shuns,
Garland for Athena's sons,
May the olive long be ours,
None may break its sacred bowers,
None its boughs of silvery grey
Young or old may bear away:
Morian Jove, with look of love,
Ever guards it from above,
Blue-eyed Pallas watch unsleeping
O'er her favourite tree is keeping.

   Swell the song of praise again ;
Other boons demand my strain,
Other blessings we inherit,
Granted by the mighty Spirit ;
On the sea and on the shore,
Ours the bridle and the oar.
Son of Saturn old ! whose sway
Stormy winds and waves obey,
Thine be honour's well-earned meed,
Tamer of the champing steed :
First he wore on Attic plain
Bit of steel and curbing rein.
Oft too o'er the waters blue,
Athens, strain thy labouring crew ;
Practised hands the bark are plying,
Oars are bending, spray is flying,
Sunny waves beneath them glancing,
Sportive Nereids round them dancing,
With their hundred feet in motion,
Twinkling mid the foam of ocean.

J. ANSTICE.

ŒDIPUS COLONEUS.

1211—1248.

ὅστις τοῦ πλέονος μέρους   στρ.
χρῄζει τοῦ μετρίου παρεὶς
ζώειν, σκαιοσύναν φυλάσσων
ἐν ἐμοὶ κατάδηλος ἔσται.
ἐπεὶ πολλὰ μὲν αἱ μακραὶ
ἁμέραι κατέθεντο δὴ
λύπας ἐγγυτέρω, τὰ τέρ-
ποντα δ' οὐκ ἂν ἴδοις ὅπου,
ὅταν τις ἐς πλέον πέσῃ
τοῦ θέλοντος· ὁ δ' ἐπίκουρος ἰσοτέλεστος,
Ἄϊδος ὅτε Μοῖρ' ἀνυμέναιος
ἄλυρος ἄχορος ἀναπέφηνε,
θάνατος ἐς τελευτάν.

μὴ φῦναι τὸν ἅπαντα νι-   ἀντ.
κᾷ λόγον· τὸ δ', ἐπεὶ φανῇ,
βῆναι κεῖθεν ὅθεν περ ἥκει
πολὺ δεύτερον ὡς τάχιστα.
ὡς εὖτ' ἂν τὸ νέον παρῇ
κούφας ἀφροσύνας φέρον,
τίς πλάγχθη πολύμοχθος ἔ-
ξω, τίς οὐ καμάτων ἔνι;
φόνοι, στάσεις, ἔρις, μάχαι,
καὶ φθόνος· τό τε κατάμεμπτον ἐπιλέλογχε
πύματον ἀκρατὲς ἀπροσόμιλον
γῆρας ἄφιλον, ἵνα πρόπαντα
κακὰ κακῶν ξυνοικεῖ.

ŒDIPUS COLONEUS.

1211—1248.

WHAT man is he that yearneth
 For length unmeasured of days?
Folly mine eye discerneth
 Encompassing all his ways.
For years over-running the measure
 Shall change thee in evil wise :
Grief draweth nigh thee ; and pleasure,
 Behold, it is hid from thine eyes.
  This to their wage have they
  Which overlive their day.
And He that looseth from labour
 Doth one with other befriend,
 Whom bride nor bridesmen attend,
Song, nor sound of the tabor,
 Death, that maketh an end.

Thy portion esteem I highest,
 Who wast not ever begot ;
Thine next, being born who diest
 And straightway again art not.
With follies light as the feather
 Doth Youth to man befall ;
Then evils gather together,
  There wants not one of them all—
  Wrath, envy, discord, strife,
  The sword that seeketh life.
And sealing the sum of trouble
 Doth tottering Age draw nigh,
 Whom friends and kinsfolk fly,
Age, upon whom redouble
 All sorrows under the sky.

ἐν ᾧ τλάμων ὅδ', οὐκ ἐγὼ μόνος,   ἐπῳδ.
πάντυθεν βόρειος ὥς τις
ἀκτὰ κυματοπλὴξ χειμερία κλονεῖται,
ὡς καὶ τόνδε κατάκρας
ἱ εἰναὶ κυματοαγεῖς
ἶται κλονέουσιν ἀεὶ ξυνοῦσαι,
αἱ μὲν ἀπ' ἀελίου δυσμᾶν,
αἱ δ' ἀνατέλλοντος,
αἱ δ' ἀνὰ μέσσαν ἀκτῖν',
αἱ δὲ νυχιᾶν ἀπὸ ῥιπᾶν.

ANTIGONE.

332—375.

πολλὰ τὰ δεινὰ κοὐδὲν ἀν-   στρ. α'.
θρώπου δεινότερον πέλει.
τοῦτο καὶ πολιοῦ πέραν
πόντου χειμερίῳ νότῳ
χωρεῖ, περιβρυχίοισιν
περῶν ὑπ' οἴδμασιν,
θεῶν τε τὰν ὑπερτάταν, Γᾶν
ἄφθιτον, ἀκαμάταν ἀποτρύεται,
ἰλλομένων ἀρότρων ἔτος εἰς ἔτος,
ἱππείῳ γένει πολεῦον.

This man, as me, even so,
Have the evil days overtaken ;
And like as a cape sea-shaken
With tempest at earth's last verges
And shock of all winds that blow,
His head the seas of woe,
The thunders of awful surges
Ruining overflow ;
Blown from the fall of even,
    Blown from the dayspring forth,
Blown from the noon in heaven,
    Blown from night and the North.

            A. E. HOUSMAN.

ANTIGONE.

332—375.

MUCH is there passing strange ;
  Nothing surpassing mankind.
He it is loves to range
Over the ocean hoar,
Thorough the surges' roar,
  South winds raging behind ;

Earth, too, wears he away,
  The mother of Gods on high
Tireless, free from decay ;
With team he furrows the ground,
And the ploughs go round and round,
  As year by year goes by.

κουφονόων τε φῦλον ὀρ-   ἀντ. α'.
νίθων ἀμφιβαλὼν ἄγει,
καὶ θηρῶν ἀγρίων ἔθνη,
πόντου τ' εἰναλίαν φύσιν
σπείραισι δικτυοκλώστοις,
περιφραδὴς ἀνήρ·
κρατεῖ δὲ μηχαναῖς ἀγραύλου
θηρὸς ὀρεσσιβάτα, λασιαύχενά θ'
ἵππον ἀέξεται ἀμφίλοφον ζυγὸν
οὔρειόν τ' ἀκμῆτα ταῦρον.

καὶ φθέγμα καὶ ἀνεμόεν   στρ. β'.
φρόνημα καὶ ἀστυνόμους ὀργὰς ἐδι-
δάξατο καὶ δυσαύλων
πάγων ὑπαίθρεια καὶ δυσ-
ομβρα φεύγειν βέλη·
παντοπόρος ἄπορος ἐπ' οὐδὲν ἔρχεται
τὸ μέλλον· Ἅιδα μόνον
φεῦξιν οὐκ ἐπάξεται·
νόσων δ' ἀμηχάνων φυγὰς ξυμπέφρασται.

σοφόν τι τὸ μηχανόεν   ἀντ. β'.
τέχνας ὑπὲρ ἐλπίδ' ἔχων ποτὲ μὲν κακὸν,
ἄλλοτ' ἐπ' ἐσθλὸν ἕρπει,
νόμους παραιρῶν χθονὸς θεῶν τ' ἔνορκον δίκαν
ὑψίπολις ἄπολις, ὅτῳ τὸ μὴ καλὸν
ξύνεστι, τόλμας χάριν.
μήτ' ἐμοὶ παρέστιος
γένοιτο μήτ' ἴσον φρονῶν ὃς τάδ' ἔρδει.

The bird-tribes, light of mind,
   The races of beasts of prey,
And sea-fish after their kind,
Man, abounding in wiles,
Entangles in his toils
   And carries captive away.

The roamers over the hill,
   The field-inhabiting deer,
By craft he conquers, at will;
He bends beneath his yoke
The neck of the steed unbroke,
   And pride of the upland steer.

He has gotten him speech, and fancy breeze-betost,
   And for the state instinct of order meet;
He has found him shelter from the chilling frost
   Of a clear sky, and from the arrowy sleet;
Illimitable in cunning, cunning-less
   He meets no change of fortune that can come;
He has found escape from pain and helplessness;
   Only he knows no refuge from the tomb.

Now bends he to the good, now to the ill,
   With craft of art, subtle past reach of sight;
Wresting his country's laws to his own will,
   Spurning the sanctions of celestial right;
High in the city, he is made city-less,
   Whoso is corrupt, for his impiety;
He that will work the works of wickedness,
   Let him not house, let him not hold, with me.

Sir George Young.

ANTIGONE.

583—625.

εὐδαίμονες οἷσι κακῶν ἄγευστος αἰών.   στρ. α΄.
οἷς γὰρ ἂν σεισθῇ θεόθεν δόμος, ἄτας
οὐδὲν ἐλλείπει, γενεᾶς ἐπὶ πλῆθος ἕρπον·
ὅμοιον ὥστε ποντίαις
οἶδμα δυσπνόοις ὅταν
Θρήσσαισιν ἔρεβος ὕφαλον ἐπιδράμῃ πνοαῖς,
κυλίνδει βυσσόθεν κελαινὰν
θῖνα καὶ δυσάνεμον,
στόνῳ βρέμουσι δ᾽ ἀντιπλῆγες ἀκταί.

ἀρχαῖα τὰ Λαβδακιδᾶν οἴκων ὁρῶμαι   ἀντ. α΄.
πήματα φθιτῶν ἐπὶ πήμασι πίπτοντ᾽,
οὐδ᾽ ἀπαλλάσσει γενεὰν γένος, ἀλλ᾽ ἐρείπει
θεῶν τις, οὐδ᾽ ἔχει λύσιν.
νῦν γὰρ ἐσχάτας ὑπὲρ
ῥίζας ὃ τέτατο φάος ἐν Οἰδίπου δόμοις,
κατ᾽ αὖ νιν φοινία θεῶν τῶν
νερτέρων ἀμᾷ κοπίς,
λόγου τ᾽ ἄνοια καὶ φρενῶν Ἐρινύς.

τεάν, Ζεῦ, δύνασιν τίς ἀνδρῶν   στρ. β΄.
ὑπερβασία κατάσχῃ;
† τὰν οὔθ᾽ ὕπνος αἱρεῖ ποθ᾽ ὁ παντογήρως
οὔτ᾽ ἄκοποι θεῶν νιν
μῆνες, ἀγήρῳ δὲ χρόνῳ δυνάστας
κατέχεις Ὀλύμπου
μαρμαρόεσσαν αἴγλαν.

ANTIGONE.

583—625.

HIGH is their happiness whose life stands clear
    From touch or taste of ill.
For them whose roof-tree rocks beneath the wrath divine,
    No respite is from fear ;
But curse on curse comes crowding on them still—
Birth after birth, their generations pine.

As when, beneath the North Wind's stormy scourge
Of bitter blasts that blow from Thracian land,
Over the deep-sea darkness drives the surge,
From the dim gulf it stirs the dark and storm-vext sand,
    And wave-worn headland and confronting shore
    Reverberate the roar ;

So see I woe on woe, ordained of old—
Woes of the living race, on woes of old time rolled,
    For all the line of Labdacus !
    No generation's blight
Can sate the curse nor give back light
Where some dark power impends, with ruin fraught !
    Awhile, light seemed to grow
O'er thy last root, O house of Œdipus !
But the fell sickle of the gods below—
Wild words and frenzy of the mind distraught—
    Hews all away to nought.

    Zeus ! by no sin of man the overbold
    Is thine high rule controlled :
    Not minished is thy strength sublime
By sleep, that preys on all, or tireless months of time !
    Ageless in power, thy living royalty
Dwells in Olympian sheen, in gleaming halls of sky !

τό τ' ἔπειτα καὶ τὸ μέλλον
καὶ τὸ πρὶν ἐπαρκέσει
† νόμος ὅδ' [οὐδὲν ἕρπων]
θνατῶν βιότῳ πάμπολις [ἐκτὸς ἄτας].

ἁ γὰρ δὴ πολύπλαγκτος ἐλπὶς   ἀντ. β'.
πολλοῖς μὲν ὄνασις ἀνδρῶν,
πολλοῖς δ' ἀπάτα κουφονόων ἐρώτων·
εἰδότι δ' οὐδὲν ἕρπει,
πρὶν πυρὶ θερμῷ πόδα τις προσαύσῃ.
σοφίᾳ γὰρ ἔκ του
κλεινὸν ἔπος πέφανται,
τὸ κακὸν δοκεῖν ποτ' ἐσθλὸν
τῷδ' ἔμμεν ὅτῳ φρένας
θεὸς ἄγει πρὸς ἄταν·
πράσσει δ' ὀλιγοστὸν χρόνον ἐκτὸς ἄτας.

ANTIGONE.
781—800.

Ἔρως ἀνίκατε μάχαν,   στρ. α'.
Ἔρως, ὃς ἐν κτήμασι πίπτεις,
ὃς ἐν μαλακαῖς παρειαῖς
νεάνιδος ἐννυχεύεις,
φοιτᾷς δ' ὑπερπόντιος ἔν τ' ἀγρονόμοις αὐλαῖς·
καί σ' οὔτ' ἀθανάτων φύξιμος οὐδεὶς
οὔθ' ἀμερίων ἐπ' ἀνθρώπων, ὁ δ' ἔχων μέμηνεν.

σὺ καὶ δικαίων ἀδίκους   ἀντ. α'.
φρένας παρασπᾷς ἐπὶ λώβᾳ·
σὺ καὶ τόδε νεῖκος ἀνδρῶν
ξύναιμον ἔχεις ταράξας·
νικᾷ δ' ἐναργὴς βλεφάρων ἵμερος εὐλέκτρου
†νύμφας, τῶν μεγάλων οὐχὶ πάρεδρος
θεσμῶν. ἄμαχος γὰρ ἐμπαίζει θεὸς Ἀφροδίτα.

This law of days long past
For the next hour and for all time stands fast—
   Who gaineth bliss or wealth too great,
    For him lurks evil fate.

Restless beguiling hope
For many men holds gladness in its scope,
But foils, for many, all they craved and sought
   In giddy pride of thought :
Man knows not fate's approach, but onward fares,
Till on the scorching fire his foot treads unawares.

Wisely one spake this immemorial word—
The man whom God unto ill doom doth lead,
Sees and is blind, deems right the wrongful deed :
And brief his date is, and his doom assured.

E. D. A. MORSHEAD.

ANTIGONE.

781—800.

O LOVE, thou art victor in fight : thou mak'st all things
   afraid ;
Thou couchest thee softly at night on the cheeks of a maid ;
Thou passest the bounds of the sea, and the folds of the
   fields ;
To thee the immortal, to thee the ephemeral yields ;
Thou maddenest them that possess thee ; thou turnest
   astray
The souls of the just, to oppress them, out of the way ;
Thou hast kindled amongst us pride, and the quarrel of kin ;
Thou art lord, by the eyes of a bride, and the love-light
   therein ;
Thou sittest assessor with Right ; her kingdom is thine,
Who sports with invincible might, Aphrodita divine.

SIR GEORGE YOUNG.

ANTIGONE.

1115—1154.

πολυώνυμε, Καδμείας Νύμφας ἄγαλμα,   στρ. α΄.
καὶ Διὸς βαρυβρεμέτα
γένος, κλυτὰν ὃς ἀμφέπεις
Ἰταλίαν, μέδεις δὲ
παγκοίνοις Ἐλευσινίας
Δηοῦς ἐν κόλποις, Βακχεῦ, Βακχᾶν
ὁ ματρόπολιν Θήβαν
ναιετῶν παρ' ὑγρῶν
Ἰσμηνοῦ ῥείθρων, ἀγρίου τ'
ἐπὶ σπορᾷ δράκοντος·

σὲ δ' ὑπὲρ διλόφοιο πέτρας στέροψ ὄπωπε   ἀντ. α΄.
λιγνύς, ἔνθα Κωρύκιαι
Νύμφαι στίχουσι Βακχίδες,
Κασταλίας τε νᾶμα·
καί σε Νυσαίων ὀρέων
κισσήρεις ὄχθαι χλωρά τ' ἀκτὰ
πολυστάφυλος πέμπει
ἀβρότων ἐπέων
εὐαζόντων Θηβαίας
ἐπισκοποῦντ' ἀγυιάς·

τὰν ἔκπαγλα τιμᾷς   στρ. β΄.
ὑπὲρ πασᾶν πόλεων
ματρὶ σὺν κεραυνίᾳ·
καὶ νῦν, ὡς βιαίας ἔχεται
πάνδαμος ἁμὰ πόλις ἐπὶ νόσου,
μολεῖν καθαρσίῳ ποδὶ Παρ-
νασίαν ὑπὲρ κλιτὺν,
ἢ στονόεντα πορθμόν.

ANTIGONE.

1115—1154.

O GOD of many a name !
Filling the heart of that Cadmeian bride
With deep delicious pride,
Offspring of him who wields the withering flame !
Thou for Italia's good
Dost care, and 'midst the all-gathering bosom wide
Of Deô dost preside :
Thou, Bacchus, by Ismenus' winding waters
'Mongst Thebè's frenzied daughters,
Keep'st haunt, commanding the fierce dragon's brood.

Thee o'er the forkèd hill
The pitchy flame beholds, where Bacchai rove,
Nymphs of Corycian grove,
Hard by the flowing of Castalia's rill.
To visit Theban ways,
By bloomy wine-cliffs flushing tender bright
'Neath far Nyseian height
Thou movest o'er the ivy-mantled mound,
While myriad voices sound
Loud strains of "Evoe!" to thy deathless praise.

For Thebè thou dost still uphold,
First of cities manifold,
Thou and the nymph whom lightning made
Mother of thy radiant head.
Come then with healing for the violent woe
That o'er our peopled land doth largely flow,
Passing the high Parnassian steep
Or moaning narrows of the deep !

ἰὼ πῦρ πνεόντων
χοράς' ἄστρων, νυχίων
φθεγμάτων ἐπίσκοπε,
παῖ Ζηνὸς γένεθλον, προφάνηθ'
ὦ Ναξίαις σαῖς ἅμα περιπόλοις
Θυίαισιν, αἲ σε μαινόμεναι
πάννυχοι χορεύουσι,
τὸν ταμίαν Ἴακχον.

Come, leader of the starry quire,
Quick-panting with their breath of fire !
Lord of high voices of the night,
Child born to him who dwells in light,
Appear with those who, joying in their madness,
Honour the sole dispenser of their gladness,
Thyiads of the Ægean main
Night-long tripping in thy train.

LEWIS CAMPBELL.

EURIPIDES.

MEDEA.

627—662.

ἔρωτες ὑπὲρ μὲν ἄγαν   στρ. α΄.
ἐλθόντες οὐκ εὐδοξίαν
οὐδ' ἀρετὰν παρέδωκαν
ἀνδράσιν· εἰ δ' ἅλις ἔλθοι
Κύπρις, οὐκ ἄλλα θεὺς εὔχαρις οὕτω.
μήποτ', ὦ δέσποιν', ἐπ' ἐμοὶ
χρυσέων τόξων ἐφείης
ἱμέρῳ χρίσασ' ἄφυκτον οἰστόν.

στέργοι δέ με σωφροσύνα,   ἀντ. α΄.
δώρημα κάλλιστον θεῶν·
μηδέ ποτ' ἀμφιλόγους ὀρ-
γὰς ἀκόρεστά τε νείκη
θυμὸν ἐκπλήξασ' ἑτέροις ἐπὶ λέκτροις
προσβάλοι δεινὰ Κύπρις, ἀ-
πτολέμους δ' εὐνὰς σεβίζουσ'
ὀξύφρων κρίνοι λέχη γυναικῶν.

ὦ πατρίς, ὦ δῶμά τ' ἐμὸν,   στρ. β΄.
μὴ δῆτ' ἄπολις γενοίμαν
τὸν ἀμαχανίας ἔχουσα
δυσπέρατον αἰῶν'
οἰκτροτάτων ἀχέων.
θανάτῳ θανάτῳ πάρος δαμείην
ἁμέραν τάνδ' ἐξανύσασα· μόχθων δ' οὐκ ἄλλος ὕπερθεν ἢ
γᾶς πατρίας στέρεσθαι.

MEDEA.

627—662.

LOVE, when she entereth in
To the heart of a man in her might,
Granteth him never to win
The meed of his glory aright ;
But should she come in degree,
There is none so gracious as she ;
Never, O queen. against me
Launch from thy golden bow
The arrow, nor erring nor slow,
Dipped in the deep of desire.

Me may modesty shield,
Of the gifts of the gods the flower ;
Ne'er may the dread Kypris yield
To me for my doleful dower
Wranglings of wrath, and the fire
Of a strife that the years cannot tire,
Ne'er may my mind she inspire
With a love that must not be mine,
Still be she wise to incline
To the unions of virtue and peace.

O land of my birth and my home,
Ne'er be it mine, is my prayer,
Houseless and helpless to roam,
Leading a life of despair
And a sorrowful lot alway ;
Rather, O death, for thy prey
Take me, and darken the day
Of my life in the light of the sun,
Hardship of earth is there none
Like to the loss of our land.

εἴδομεν, οὐκ ἐξ ἑτέρων　　　　　ἀντ. β'.
μύθων ἔχομεν φράσασθαι·
σὲ γὰρ οὐ πόλις, οὐ φίλων τις
ᾤκτισεν παθοῦσαν
δεινότατον παθέων.
ἀχάριστος ὄλοιθ' ὅτῳ πάρεστι
μὴ φίλους τιμᾶν, καθαρὰν ἀνοί-
ξαντα κλῇδα φρενῶν· ἐμοὶ
μὲν φίλος οὔποτ' ἔσται.

HIPPOLYTUS.

525—564.

Ἔρως Ἔρως, ὃ κατ' ὀμμάτων　　　　　στρ. α'.
στάζεις πόθον, εἰσάγων γλυκεῖαν
ψυχᾷ χάριν οὓς ἐπιστρατεύσῃ,
μή μοί ποτε σὺν κακῷ φανείης,
μηδ' ἄρρυθμος ἔλθοις.
οὔτε γὰρ πυρὸς οὔτ'
ἄστρων ὑπέρτερον βέλος
οἷον τὸ τᾶς Ἀφροδίτας
ἵησιν ἐκ χερῶν
Ἔρως, ὁ Διὸς παῖς.

ἄλλως ἄλλως παρά τ' Ἀλφεῷ　　　　　ἀντ. α'.
Φοίβου τ' ἐπὶ Πυθίοις τερέμνοις
βούταν φόνον Ἑλλὰς αἶ' ἀέξει·
Ἔρωτα δέ, τὸν τύραννον ἀνδρῶν,
τὸν τᾶς Ἀφροδίτας
φιλτάτων θαλάμων
κλῃδοῦχον, οὐ σεβίζομεν,
πέρθοντα καὶ διὰ πάσας
ἰόντα συμφορᾶς
θνατοῖς, ὅταν ἔλθῃ.

This do I know of a truth,
Not from report is the tale
That I ponder ; pity nor ruth
For thy burden of bale
From city or friend hast thou
To solace thy suffering now ;
Perish the ingrate, I trow,
Who never at friendship's behest
Flings back the bars of his breast,
Friend is he none for me.

G. SOUTAR.

HIPPOLYTUS.

525—564.

O LOVE ! O Love ! from the eyes of thee
  Droppeth desire, and into the soul
That thou conquerest leadest thou sweetness and charm ;
  Come not to me bringing sorrow or harm,
    And come not in dole,
Nor with measureless passion o'ermaster thou me !
    For neither the lightning fire
    Nor the bolts of the stars are dire
As the dart hurled forth from the hand of Love,
    The Son of God above.

  For vainly, vainly, and all in vain
Pile we to Phœbus the Pythian shrines ;
  Vainly by Alpheus heap victims on high ;
  Vain indeed are the prayers we cry,
    If no prayer divines
That Love is the tyrant and master of men.
    Through every fate he errs,
    The keeper of bride-chambers,
Nor alike unto all, nor one only way,
  He comes to spoil and slay.

τὰν μεν Οἰχαλία   στρ. β΄.
πῶλον, ἄζυγα λέκτρων,
ἄνανδρον τὸ πρὶν καὶ ἄνυμφον, οἴκων
ζεύξασ' ἄπ' εἰρεσίᾳ, δρομάδα
τὰν Ἄϊδος ὥστε βάκχαν,
σὺν αἵματι, σὺν καπνῷ
φονίοις θ' ὑμεναίοισιν
Ἀλκμήνας τόκῳ Κύπρις ἐξέδωκεν·
ὦ τλάμων ὑμεναίων.

ὦ Θήβας ἱερὸν   ἀντ. β΄.
τεῖχος, ὦ στόμα Δίρκας,
συνείποιτ' ἄν ἀ Κύπρις οἷον ἕρπει.
βροντᾷ γὰρ ἀμφιπύρῳ τοκάδα
τὰν Διογόνοιο Βάκχου
νυμφευσαμέναν πότμῳ
φονίῳ κατεκοίμασε.
δεινὰ γὰρ τὰ πάντ' ἐπιπνεῖ, μέλισσα δ'
οἷα τις πεπόταται.

ALCESTIS.

435—454.

ὦ Πελίου θύγατερ,
χαίρουσά μοι εἰν Ἀΐδα δόμοισι
τὸν ἀνάλιον οἶκον οἰκετεύοις.
ἴστω δ' Ἀΐδας ὁ μελιγχαίτας
θεός, ὅς τ' ἐπὶ κώπᾳ
πηδαλίῳ τε γέρων
νεκροπομπὸς ἵζει,
πολὺ δὴ πολὺ δὴ γυναῖκ' ἀρίσταν
λίμναν Ἀχεροντίαν πορεύ-
σας ἐλάτᾳ δικώπῳ.

Think on that Œchalian riven
Away from her home and her country, and driven,
  A maiden unwedded, across the seas,
Rushing on Hades in fury, and mad with her wrongs ;
  For Cypris gave his bride to Herakles
With blood, with smoke, with flame, with murderous
    marriage songs.

    O Theban Wall !　O mouth of Dirce !
Tell with me how without haste, without mercy,
Into the soul doth Cypris creep ;
Witness of Semele wed in a death-bringing hour
With fire, with thunder, sent to her last sleep,
And of Love, more restless than bees, inspiring all with
    his power.
A. MARY F. ROBINSON.
(Madame Darmesteter.)

ALCESTIS.

435—454.

FARE thee well, good and fair, Pelias's noble heir,
    Thy course is done ;
  Good and gracious things betide thee,
  In the dark mansion that must hide thee
    From yon fair sun.
The Sovereign of the Realm, and he that at the Helm
Steers in the murky stream his dusky wherry,
(Wafting the feeble sprites that flit below,)
    Shall hear and know,
  That never did a nobler spirit pass
    The Infernal Ferry.

πολλά σε μουσοπόλοι
μέλψουσι καθ᾿ ἑπτάτονόν τ᾿ ὀρείαν
χέλυν ἔν τ᾿ ἀλύροις κλέοντες ὕμνοις,
Σπάρτᾳ κυκλὰς ἁνίκα Καρνείου περινίσσεται ὥρα
μηνὸς ἀειρομένας
παννύχου σελάνας,
λιπαραῖσί τ᾿ ἐν ὀλβίαις Ἀθάναις.
τοίαν ἔλιπες θανοῦσα μολ-
πὰν μελέων ἀοιδοῖς.

ALCESTIS.
567—605.

ὦ πολύξεινος καὶ ἐλεύθερος ἀνδρὸς ἀεί ποτ᾿ οἶκος,
σέ τοι καὶ ὁ Πύθιος εὐλύρας Ἀπόλλων
ἠξίωσε ναίειν,
ἔτλα δὲ σοῖσι μηλονόμας
ἐν δόμοις γενέσθαι,
δοχμιᾶν διὰ κλιτύων
βοσκήμασι σοῖσι συρίζων
ποιμνίτας ὑμεναίους.

σὺν δ᾿ ἐποιμαίνοντο χαρᾷ μελέων βαλιαί τε λύγκες   ἀντ.
ἔβα δὲ λιποῦσ᾿ Ὄθρυος νάπαν λεόντων
ἁ δαφοινὸς ἴλα·
χόρευσε δ᾿ ἀμφὶ σὰν κιθάραν,
Φοῖβε, ποικιλόθριξ
νεβρὸς ὑψικόμων πέραν
βαίνουσ᾿ ἐλατᾶν σφυρῷ κούφῳ,
χαίρουσ᾿ εὔφρονι μολπᾷ.

Firm and fond, far, far beyond
The best of woman-kind that have been ever ;
    Whilst here on earth above,
    Thy constant worth and love,
Shall form the theme of emulous endeavour,
Wherever minstrels sing—or where they strike the string ;
    Whether in Sparta's ancient state austere,
      When the revolving year
Brings round the high Karneian festival,
And the moon's awful and full orbèd ball
      Fills and illumines all :
Or where proud Athens hails the festive day,
With pomp and art and prosperous display.

              JOHN HOOKHAM FRERE.

ALCESTIS.

567—605.

HAIL ! House of the open door,
    Hail ! home of the chieftain free !
The Lord of the Lyre himself of yore
    Deign'd to inhabit thee.
In thy halls, disguised in his shepherd's weeds,
    He endured for a while to stay,
      Through the upland rocks,
      To the feeding flocks,
Piping the pastoral lay.

And the spotted Lynx was tame
    With the joy of the mighty spell ;
And, a tawny troop, the Lions came
    From the leafy Othrys dell ;
And from where the tall pines waved their locks,
    Still as the lute would play,
      Light tripp'd the Fawn
      O'er the level lawn,
Entranced by the genial lay.

τοιγὰρ πολυμηλοτάταν   στρ.
ἑστίαν οἰκεῖ παρὰ καλλίναον
Βοιβίαν λίμναν· ἀρότοις δὲ γυᾶν
καὶ πεδίων δαπέδοις ὅρον ἀμφὶ μὲν ἀελίου κνεφαίαν
ἱππόστασιν αἰθέρα τὰν Μολοσσῶν τίθεται,
πόντιον δ' Αἰγαίων' ἐπ' ἀκτὰν
ἀλίμενον Πηλίου κρατύνει.

καὶ νῦν δόμον ἀμπετάσας   ἀντ.
δέξετο ξεῖνον νοτερῷ βλεφάρῳ,
τᾶς φίλας κλαίων ἀλόχου νέκυν ἐν
δώμασιν ἀρτιθανῆ· τὸ γὰρ εὐγενὲς ἐκφέρεται πρὸς αἰδῶ.
ἐν τοῖς ἀγαθοῖσι δὲ πάντ' ἔνεστιν σοφίας.
πρὸς δ' ἐμᾷ ψυχᾷ θάρσος ἧσται
θεοσεβῆ φῶτα κεδνὰ πράξειν.

ALCESTIS.
962—1005.

ἐγὼ καὶ διὰ μούσας   στρ.
καὶ μετάρσιος ᾖξα, καὶ
πλείστων ἀψάμενος λόγων
κρεῖσσον οὐδὲν ἀνάγκας
ηὗρον, οὐδέ τι φάρμακον
Θρήσσαις ἐν σανίσιν, τὰς
Ὀρφεία κατέγραψεν
γῆρυς, οὐδ' ὅσα Φοῖβος Ἀσ-
κληπιάδαις ἔδωκε
φάρμακα πολυπόνοις
ἀντιτεμὼν βροτοῖσιν.

The house where the Lord Admetus bides
   Is blest for the Pythian's sake—
Fast by the shores that skirt the tides
   Of the pleasant Bœbian Lake.
His fallows and fields the Molossians bound
To the stall of the Steeds of Day,—
     And to airy sweep
     Of Ægean steep
All Pelion owns his sway.

He will welcome the stranger with moisten'd lid
   Though his hall he hath open'd wide ;
Wailing the dead in his chamber hid,
   The love that hath lately died.
For the noble-born is on high thoughts bent,
   And the good are the truly wise ;
     And deep in my breast
     Doth the firm faith rest,
That his hopes from the dust will rise.

               T. E. WEBB.

ALCESTIS.

962—1005.

IN heaven-high musings and many,
   Far-seeking and deep debate,
Of strong things find I not any
   That is as the strength of Fate.
Help nor healing is told
In soothsayings uttered of old,
In the Thracian runes, the verses
   Engraven of Orpheus' pen ;
No balm of virtue to save
Apollo aforetime gave,
Who stayeth with tender mercies
   The plagues of the children of men.

μόνας δ' οὔτ' ἐπὶ βωμοὺς   ἀντ.
ἐλθεῖν οὔτε βρέτας θεᾶς
ἔστιν, οὐ σφαγίων κλύει.
μή μοι, πότνια, μείζων
ἔλθοις ἢ τὸ πρὶν ἐν βίῳ.
καὶ γὰρ Ζεὺς ὅ τι νεύσῃ,
σὺν σοὶ τοῦτο τελευτᾷ.
καὶ τὸν ἐν Χαλύβοις δαμά-
ζεις σὺ βίᾳ σίδαρον,
οὐδέ τις ἀποτόμου
λήματός ἐστιν αἰδώς.

καί σ' ἐν ἀφύκτοισι χερῶν   στρ.
εἷλε θεὰ δεσμοῖς·
τόλμα δ'· οὐ γὰρ ἀνάξεις ποτ' ἔνερθεν
κλαίων τοὺς φθιμένους ἄνω.
καὶ θεῶν σκότιοι φθίνουσι
παῖδες ἐν θανάτῳ.
φίλα μὲν ὅτ' ἦν μεθ' ἡμῶν,
φίλα δ' ἔτι καὶ θανοῦσα·
γενναιοτάταν δὲ πασᾶν
ἐζεύξω κλισίαις ἄκοιτιν.

μηδὲ νεκρῶν ὡς φθιμένων   ἀντ.
χῶμα νομιζέσθω
τύμβος σᾶς ἀλόχου, θεοῖσι δ' ὁμοίως
τιμάσθω, σέβας ἐμπόρων.
καί τις δοχμίαν κέλευθον
ἐμβαίνων τόδ' ἐρεῖ·
αὕτα ποτὲ προὔθαν' ἀνδρός,
νῦν δ' ἐστὶ μάκαιρα δαίμων,
χαῖρ', ὦ πότνι', εὖ δὲ δοίης.
τοῖαί νιν προσεροῦσι φᾶμαι.

She hath not her habitation
   In temples that hands have wrought ;
Him that bringeth oblation,
   Behold, she heedeth him naught.
Be thou not wroth with us more,
O mistress, than heretofore ;
For what God willeth soever,
   That thou bringest to be ;
Thou breakest in sunder the brand
Far forged in the Iron Land ;
Thine heart is cruel, and never
   Came pity anigh unto thee.

Thee too, O King, hath she taken
   And bound in her tenfold chain ;
   Yet faint not, neither complain :
The dead thou wilt not awaken
   For all thy weeping again.
They perish, whom gods begot ;
The night releaseth them not.
Beloved was she that died
And dear shall ever abide,
For this was the queen among women, Admetus, that
   lay by thy side.

Not as the multitude lowly
   Asleep in their sepulchres,
   Not as their grave be hers,
But like as the gods held holy,
   The worship of wayfarers.
Yea, all that travel the way
Far off shall see it and say,
Lo, erst for her lord she died,
To-day she sitteth enskied ;
Hail, lady, be gracious to usward ; that alway her honour
   abide.

              A. E. HOUSMAN.

HELENA.

1451—1511.

Φοίνισσα Σιδωνιὰς ὦ   στρ.
ταχεῖα κώπα, ῥοθίοισι μάτηρ,
εἰρεσίᾳ φίλα,
χοραγὲ τῶν καλλιχόρων
δελφίνων, ὅταν αὔραις
πέλαγος νήνεμον ᾖ,
γλαυκὰ δὲ Πόντου θυγάτηρ
Γαλάνεια τάδ᾽ εἴπῃ·
κατὰ μὲν ἱστία πετάσατ᾽ αὔραις
λείποντες εἰναλίαις,
λάβετε δ᾽ εἰλατίνας πλάτας,
ἰὼ ναῦται, ἰὼ ναῦται,
πέμποντες εὐλιμένους
Περσείων οἴκων Ἑλέναν ἐπ᾽ ἀκτάς.

ἦ που κόρας ἂν ποταμοῦ   ἀντ.
παρ᾽ οἶδμα Λευκιππίδας, ἢ πρὸ ναοῦ
Παλλάδος ἂν λάβοις
χρόνῳ ξυνελθοῦσα χοροῖς
ἢ κώμοις Ὑακίνθου
νυχίαν εὐφροσύνάν
(ὃν ἐξαμιλλησάμενος
τροχῷ τέρμονι δίσκου
ἔκανε Φοῖβος, ὅθεν Λακαίνᾳ γᾷ
βούθυτον ἁμέραν
ὁ Διὸς εἶπε σέβειν γόνος),
μόσχον θ᾽, ἃν λιπέτην οἴκοις
[θάλλουσαν ἐν θαλάμοις],
ἃς οὔπω πεῦκαι πρὸ γάμων ἔλαμψαν.

√.

HELENA.

1451—1511.

FAIR be thy speed, Sidonian ship !
Thine oars, familiar to the oarsman's grip,
    Fall fast, and make the surges bound,
    And lead along the dolphin train,
        While all around
    The winds forego to vex the main,
        And the mariners hear
    The sea-king's daughter calling clear,
" Now, sails to the breeze, fling out, fling out,
Now pull, strong arms, to the cheering shout ;
Speed royal Helen, away and away,
To Argos home, to the royal bay."

    What sacred hour, what festal tide
Shall bring fair Helen to Eurotas' side ?
    Say, shall the Spartan maidens dance
    Before Leucippis then ?   Or meet
        That day perchance
    At Pallas' gate ?   Or shall they greet
        Thee, lost so long,
    With lost Hyacinthus' nightly song,
How Phœbus slew him with quoit far-flown,
And yearly the maidens with mourning atone ?
There is one of them, Helen, one fair of the fair,
Who will not be wife till her mother be there !

H

δι' ἀέρος εἴθε ποτανοὶ   στρ.
γενοίμεθ' ὅθι στολάδες
οἰωνοὶ Λίβυες
ὄμβρον χειμέριον λιποῦσαι
νίσσονται πρεσβυτάτᾳ
σύριγγι πειθόμεναι
ποιμένος, ὃς ἄβροχα πεδία καρποφόρα τε γᾶς
ἐπιπετόμενος ἰακχεῖ.
ὦ πταναὶ δολιχαύχενες,
σύννομοι νεφέων δρόμου,
βᾶτε Πλειάδας ὑπὸ μέσας
Ὠρίωνά τ' ἐννύχιον,
καρύξατ' ἀγγελίαν,
Εὐρώταν ἐφεζόμεναι,
Μενέλεως ὅτι Δαρδάνου
πόλιν ἑλὼν δόμον ἥξει.

μόλοιτέ ποθ' ἵππιον ἅρμα   ἀντ.
δι' αἰθέρος ἱέμενοι
παῖδες Τυνδαρίδαι,
λαμπρῶν ὑπ' ἄστρων ὑπ' ἀέλλαισι
ναίετ' οὐράνιοι,
σωτῆρες τᾶς Ἑλένας
γλαυκὸν ὑπὲρ οἶδμα κυανόχροά τε κυμάτων
ῥόθια πολιὰ θαλάσσας,
ναύταις εὐαεῖς ἀνέμων
πέμποντες Διόθεν πνοάς·
δύσκλειαν δ' ἀπὸ συγγόνου
βάλετε βαρβάρων λεχέων,
ἃν Ἰδαίων ἐρίδων
ποιναθεῖσ' ἐκτήσατο, γᾶν
οὐκ ἐλθοῦσά ποτ' Ἰλίου
Φοιβείους ἐπὶ πύργους.

O for wings to fly
Where the flocks of fowl together
Quit the Afric sky,
Late their refuge from the wintry weather !
All the way with solemn sound
Rings the leader's clarion cry
O'er dewless deserts and glad harvest-ground.
We would bid them, as they go,
Neck by neck against the cloud
Racing nightly neath the stars,
When Eurotas rolls below,
Light and leave a message loud,
How princely Menelaus, proud
With conquest, cometh from the Dardan wars.

Come, eternal Pair,
Come, Twin Brethren, from your heaven ascended ;
Down the steep of air
Drive, by many a starry glance attended !
Mid the waters white and blue,
Mid the rolling waves be there,
And brotherly bring safe your sister through.
Airs from heaven, serene and pure,
Breathe upon her ; bless and speed ;
Breathe away her cruel shame !
Never her did Paris lure,
Never won her (as they rede)
Of Aphroditè for his meed,
Nor thither led, where never yet she came !

A. W. Verrall.

HERCULES FURENS.

348—441.

αἴλινον μὲν ἐπ' εὐτυχεῖ   στρ.
μολπᾷ Φοῖβος ἰακχεῖ,
τὰν καλλίφθογγον κιθάραν
ἐλαύνων πλήκτρῳ χρυσέῳ·
ἐγὼ δὲ τὸν γᾶς ἐνέρων τ' ἐς ὄρφναν
μολόντα, παῖδ' εἴτε Διός νιν εἴπω
εἴτ' Ἀμφιτρύωνος ἶνιν,
ὑμνῆσαι, στεφάνωμα μό-
χθων, δι' εὐλογίας θέλω.
γενναίων δ' ἀρεταὶ πόνων
τοῖς θανοῦσιν ἄγαλμα.
πρῶτον μὲν Διὸς ἄλσος
ἠρήμωσε λέοντος,
πυρσοῦ δ' ἀμφεκαλύφθη
ξανθὸν κρᾶτ' ἐπινωτίσας
δεινῷ χάσματι θηρός·

τάν τ' ὀρεινόμον ἀγρίων   ἀντ.
Κενταύρων ποτὲ γένναν
ἔτρωσεν τόξοις φονίοις,
ἐναίρων πτανοῖς βέλεσιν.
ξύνοιδε Πηνειὸς ὁ καλλιδίνας
μακραί τ' ἄρουραι πεδίων ἄκαρποι
καὶ Πηλιάδες θεράπναι
σύγχορτοί θ' Ὁμόλας ἔναυ-
λοι, πεύκαισιν ὅθεν χέρας
πληροῦντες χθόνα Θεσσαλῶν
ἱππείαις ἐδάμαζον·

HERCULES FURENS.

348—441.

EVEN a dirge can Phoibos suit
In song to music jubilant
For all its sorrow : making shoot
His golden plectron o'er the lute,
Melodious ministrant.
And I, too, am of mind to raise,
Despite the imminence of doom,
A song of joy, outpour my praise
To him—what is it rumour says ?—
Whether—now buried in the ghostly gloom
Below ground,—he was child of Zeus indeed,
Or mere Amphitruon's mortal seed—
To him I weave the wreath of song, his labour's meed.
For, is my hero perished in the feat ?
The virtues of brave toils, in death complete,
These save the dead in song—their glory-garland meet !

First, then, he made the wood
Of Zeus a solitude,
Slaying its lion-tenant : and he spread
The tawniness behind : his yellow head
Enmuffled by the brute's, backed by that grin of dread.
The mountain-roving savage Kentaur-race
He strewed with deadly bow about their place.
Slaying with wingèd shafts : Peneios knew,
Beauteously-eddying, and the long tracts too
Of pasture trampled fruitless, and as well
Those desolated haunts Mount Pelion under,
And, grassy up to Homolè, each dell
Whence, having filled their hands with pine-tree plunder,
Horse-like was wont to prance from, and subdue
The land of Thessaly, that bestial crew.

τάν τε χρυσοκάρανον
δόρκα ποικιλόνωτον,
συλήτειραν ἀγρωστᾶν
κτείνας, θηροφόνον θεὰν
Οἰνῶατιν ἀγάλλει·

τεθρίππων τ' ἐπέβα   στρ.
καὶ ψαλίοις ἐδάμασσε πώλους
Διομήδεος, οἳ φονίαισι φάτναις ἀχάλιν' ἐθόαζον
κάθαιμα σῖτα γένυσι, χαρ-
μοναῖσιν ἀνδροβρῶσι δυστράπεζοι·
περῶν δ' ἀργυρορρύταν Ἕβρον
ἐξέπρασσε μόχθον,
Μυκηναίῳ πονῶν τυράννῳ,
τάν τε Πηλιάδ' ἀκτὰν
Ἀναύρου παρὰ πηγάς·
Κύκνον τε ξενοδαίκταν
τόξοις ὤλεσεν, Ἀμφαναί-
ας οἰκήτορ' ἄμικτον·

ὑπνῳοὺς τε κόρας   ἀντ.
ἤλυθεν ἑσπερίαν ἐς αὐλάν,
χρύσεον πετάλων ἄπο μηλοφόρων χερὶ καρπὸν ἀμέρξων,
δράκοντα πυρσόνωτον, ὅς σφ'
ἄπλατον ἀμφελικτὺς ἕλικ' ἐφρούρει,
κτανών· ποντίας θ' ἁλὸς μυχοὺς
εἰσέβαινε, θνατοῖς
γαλανείας τιθεὶς ἐρετμοῖς·
οὐρανοῦ θ' ὑπὸ μέσσαν
ἐλαύνει χέρας ἕδραν,
Ἄτλαντος δόμον ἐλθών·
ἀστρῶπους τε κατέσχεν οἴ-
κους εὐανορίᾳ θεῶν·

The golden-headed spot-back'd stag he slew,
That robber of the rustics : glorified
Therewith the goddess who in hunter's pride
Slaughters the game along Oinoë's side.
And, yoked abreast, he brought the chariot-breed
To pace submissive to the bit, each steed
That in the bloody cribs of Diomede
Champed, and, unbridled, hurried down that gore
For grain, exultant the dread feast before—
Of man's flesh : hideous feeders they of yore !
All as he crossed the Hebros' silver-flow
Accomplished he such labour, toiling so
For Mukenaian tyrant : ay, and more—
He crossed the Melian shore
And, by the sources of Amauros, shot
To death that strangers' pest
Kuknos, who dwelt in Amphanaia : not
Of fame for good to guest !

And next to the melodious maids he came,
Inside the Hesperian court-yard : hand must aim
At plucking gold fruit from the appled leaves,
Now he had killed the dragon, backed like flame,
Who guards the unapproachable : he weaves
Himself all round, one spire about the same.
And into those sea-troughs of ocean dived
The hero, and for mortals calm contrived,
Whatever oars should follow in his wake.
And under heaven's mid-seat his hands thrust he,
At home with Atlas : and, for valour's sake,
Held the gods up their star-faced mansionry.

τὸν ἱππευτάν τ᾽ Ἀμαζόνων στρατὸν   στρ.
Μαιῶτιν ἀμφὶ πολυπόταμον
ἔβα δι᾽ Εὔξεινον οἶδμα λίμνας,
τίν᾽ οὐκ ἀφ᾽ Ἑλλανίας
ἄγορον ἁλίσας φίλων,
κόρας Ἀρείας πέπλων
χρυσεόστολον φάρος,
ζωστῆρος ὀλεθρίους ἄγρας.
τὰ κλεινὰ δ᾽ Ἑλλὰς ἔλαβε βαρβάρου κόρας
λάφυρα, καὶ σώζετ᾽ ἐν Μυκήναις.
τάν τε μυριόκρανον
πολύφονον κύνα Λέρνας
ὕδραν ἐξεπύρωσεν
βέλεσί τ᾽ ἀμφέβαλλε,
τὸν τρισώματον οἶσιν ἔ-
κτα βοτῆρ᾽ Ἐρυθείας.

δρόμων τ᾽ ἄλλων ἀγάλματ᾽ εὐτυχῆ   ἀντ.
διῆλθε· τόν τε πολυδάκρυον
ἔπλευσ᾽ ἐς Ἅιδαν, πόνων τελευτὰν,
ἵν᾽ ἐκπεραίνει τάλας
βίοτον οὐδ᾽ ἔβα πάλιν.
στέγαι δ᾽ ἔρημοι φίλων,
τὰν δ᾽ ἀνόστιμον τέκνων
Χάρωνος ἐπιμένει πλάτα
βίου κέλευθον ἄθεον, ἄδικον· ἐς δὲ σὰς
χέρας βλέπει δώματ᾽ οὐ παρόντος.
εἰ δ᾽ ἐγὼ σθένος ἥβων
δόρυ τ᾽ ἔπαλλον ἐν αἰχμᾷ,
Καδμείων τε σύνηβοι,
τέκεσιν ἂν παρέσταν
ἀλκᾷ· νῦν δ᾽ ἀπολείπομαι
τᾶς εὐδαίμονος ἥβας.

Also, the rider-host of Amazons
About Maiotis many-streamed, he went
To conquer through the billowy Euxin once,
Having collected what an armament
Of friends from Hellas, all on conquest bent
Of that gold-garnished cloak, dread girdle-chase !
So Hellas gained the girl's barbarian grace
And at Mukenai saves the trophy still—
Go wonder there, who will !

And the ten thousand-headed hound
Of many a murder, the Lernaian snake
He burned out, head by head, and cast around
His darts a poison thence,—darts soon to slake
Their rage in that three-bodied herdsman's gore
Of Erutheia.   Many a running more
He made for triumph and felicity,
And, last of toils, to Haides, never dry
Of tears, he sailed : and there he, luckless, ends
His life completely, nor returns again.
The house and home are desolate of friends,
And where the children's life-path leads them, plain
I see,—no step retraceable, no god
Availing, and no law to help the lost !
The oar of Charon marks their period,
Waits to end all.   Thy hands, these roofs accost !—
To thee, though absent, look their uttermost !

But if in youth and strength I flourished still,
Still shook the spear in fight, did power match will
In these Kadmeian co-mates of my age,
They would,—and I,—when warfare was to wage,
Stand by these children ; but I am bereft
Of youth now, lone of that good genius left !

ROBERT BROWNING.

HERCULES FURENS.

637—672.

ἁ νεότας μοι φίλον· ἄχθος δὲ τὸ γῆρας ἀεὶ   στρ.
βαρύτερον Αἴτνας σκοπέλων
ἐπὶ κρατὶ κεῖται,
βλεφάρων σκοτεινὸν
φάος ἐπικαλύψαν.
μή μοι μήτ' Ἀσιάτιδος
τυραννίδος ὄλβος εἴη,
μὴ χρυσοῦ δώματα πλήρη
τᾶς ἥβας ἀντιλαβεῖν,
ἃ καλλίστα μὲν ἐν ὄλβῳ,
καλλίστα δ' ἐν πενίᾳ.
τὸ δὲ λυγρὸν φόνιόν τε γῆρας μισῶ· κατὰ κυμάτων δ'
ἔρροι, μηδέ ποτ' ὤφελεν
θνατῶν δώματα καὶ πόλεις
ἐλθεῖν, ἀλλὰ κατ' αἰθέρ' ἀ-
εὶ πτεροῖσι φορείσθω.

εἰ δὲ θεοῖς ἦν ξύνεσις καὶ σοφία κατ' ἄνδρας,   ἀντ.
δίδυμον ἂν ἥβαν ἔφερον,
φανερὸν χαρακτῆρ'
ἀρετᾶς, ὅσοισιν
μέτα, καὶ θανόντες
εἰς αὐγὰς πάλιν ἁλίου
δισσοὺς ἂν ἔβαν διαύλους,
ἁ δυσγένεια δ' ἁπλᾶν ἂν
εἶχε ζόας βιοτὰν,
καὶ τῷδ' ἂν τούς τε κακοὺς ἂν
γνῶναι καὶ τοὺς ἀγαθοὺς,
ἴσον ἅτ' ἐν νεφέλαισιν ἄ-
στρων ναύταις ἀριθμὸς πέλει.

HERCULES FURENS.

637—672.

YOUTH is a pleasant burthen to me ;
But age on my head, more heavily
Than the crags of Aitna, weighs and weighs,
And darkening cloaks the lids and intercepts the rays.
Never be mine the preference
Of an Asian empire's wealth, nor yet
Of a house all gold, to youth, to youth
That's beauty, whatever the gods dispense !
Whether in wealth we joy, or fret
Paupers,—of all God's gifts most beautiful, in truth !

But miserable murderous age I hate !
Let it go to wreck, the waves adown,
Nor ever by rights plague tower or town
Where mortals bide, but still elate
With wings, on ether, precipitate,
Wander them round—nor wait !

But if the gods, to man's degree,
Had wit and wisdom, they would bring
Mankind a twofold youth, to be
Their virtue's sign-mark, all should see,
In those with whom life's winter thus grew spring.
For when they died, into the sun once more
Would they have traversed twice life's race-course o'er ;
While ignobility had simply run
Existence through, nor second life begun.
And so might we discern both bad and good
As surely as the starry multitude
Is numbered by the sailors, one and one.

νῦν δ᾽ οὐδεὶς ὅρος ἐκ θεῶν
χρηστοῖς οὐδὲ κακοῖς σαφής,
ἀλλ᾽ εἱλισσόμενός τις αἰ-
ὼν πλοῦτον μόνον αὔξει.

BACCHÆ.

370—431.

᾽Οσία, πότνα θεῶν,   στρ.
᾽Οσία δ᾽, ἃ κατὰ γᾶν
χρυσέαν πτέρυγα φέρεις,
τάδε Πενθέως ἀΐεις,
ἀΐεις οὐχ ὁσίαν
ὕβριν ἐς τὸν Βρόμιον,
τὸν Σεμέλας τὸν παρὰ καλλιστεφάνοις
εὐφροσύναις δαίμονα πρῶ-
τον μακάρων; ὃς τάδ᾽ ἔχει,
θιασεύειν τε χοροῖς,
μετά τ᾽ αὐλοῦ γελάσαι
ἀποπαῦσαί τε μερίμνας,
ὁπόταν βότρυος ἔλθῃ
γάνος ἐν δαιτὶ θεῶν,
κισσοφόροις δ᾽ ἐν θαλίαις
ἀνδράσι κρατὴρ ὕπνον ἀμφιβάλλῃ.

ἀχαλίνων στομάτων   ἀντ.
ἀνόμου τ᾽ ἀφροσύνας
τὸ τέλος δυστυχία·
ὁ δὲ τᾶς ἡσυχίας
βίοτος καὶ τὸ φρονεῖν
ἀσάλευτόν τε μένει
καὶ συνέχει δώματα· πόρσω γὰρ ὅμως
αἰθέρα ναίοντες ὁρῶ-
σιν τὰ βροτῶν οὐρανίδαι.

But now the gods by no apparent line
Limit the worthy and the base define ;
Only, a certain period rounds, and so
Brings man more wealth—but youthful vigour, no !

ROBERT BROWNING.

BACCHÆ.

370—431.

HOLY Goddess ! Goddess old !
Holy ! thou the crown of gold
In the nether realm that wearest,
Pentheus' awful speech thou hearest,
Hearest his insulting tone
'Gainst Semelè's immortal son,
Bromius, of Gods the first and best.
At every gay and flower-crowned feast,
His the dance's jocund strife,
And the laughter with the fife,
Every care and grief to lull,
When the sparkling wine-cup full
Crowns the gods' banquet, or lets fall
Sweet sleep on the eyes of men at mortal festival.

Of tongue unbridled without awe,
Of madness spurning holy law,
Sorrow is the Jove-doomed close ;
But the life of calm repose
And modest reverence holds her state
Unbroken by disturbing fate ;
And knits whole houses in the tie
Of sweet domestic harmony.

τὸ σοφὸν δ' οὐ σοφία,
τό τε μὴ θνατὰ φρονεῖν.
βραχὺς αἰών· ἐπὶ τούτῳ
δέ τις ἂν μεγάλα διώκων
τὰ παρόντ' οὐχὶ φέροι.
μαινομένων οἵδε τρόποι
καὶ κακοβούλων παρ' ἔμοιγε φωτῶν.

ἱκοίμαν ποτὶ Κύπρον,   στρ.
νᾶσον τᾶς Ἀφροδίτας,
ἵν' οἱ θελξίφρονες νέμον-
ται θνατοῖσιν Ἔρωτες,
Πάφον θ', ἃν ἑκατύστομοι
βαρβάρου ποταμοῦ ῥοαὶ
καρπίζουσιν ἄνομβροι.
ὅπου καλλιστευομένα
Πιερία μούσειος ἕδρα,
σεμνὰ κλιτὺς Ὀλύμπου,
ἐκεῖσ' ἆγε με, Βρόμιε Βρόμιε,
προβακχήιε δαῖμον·
ἐκεῖ χάριτες, ἐκεῖ δὲ πόθος·
ἐκεῖ δὲ βάκχαισι θέμις ὀργιάζειν.

ὁ δαίμων ὁ Διὸς παῖς   ἀντ.
χαίρει μὲν θαλίαισιν,
φιλεῖ δ' ὀλβοδότειραν Εἰ-
ρήναν, κουροτρόφον θεάν.
ἴσαν δ' ἔς τε τὸν ὄλβιον
τόν τε χείρονα δῶκ' ἔχειν
οἴνου τέρψιν ἄλυπον·
μισεῖ δ' ᾧ μὴ ταῦτα μέλει,
κατὰ φάος νύκτας τε φίλας
εὐαίωνα διαζῆν·

Beyond the range of mortal eyes
'Tis not wisdom to be wise,
Life is brief, the present clasp,
Nor after some bright future grasp,
Such were the wisdom, as I ween
Only of frantic and ill-counselled men.

O, would to Cyprus I might roam,
 Soft Aphrodite's isle,
Where the young Loves have their perennial home,
 That soothe men's hearts with tender guile :
Or to that wondrous shore, where ever
The hundred-mouthed barbaric river
Makes teem with wealth the showerless land !
O lead me ! lead me, till I stand,
Bromius ! sweet Bromius ! where high swelling
Soars the Pierian Muses' dwelling—
Olympus' summit hoar and high—
Thou revel-loving Deity !
 For there are all the Graces,
  And sweet Desire is there,
  And to those hallowed places,
To lawful rites the Bacchanals repair.

The Deity, the son of Jove,
 The banquet is his joy,
Peace, the wealth-giver, doth he love,
 That nurse of many a noble boy.
Not the rich man's sole possessing ;
To the poor the painless blessing
Gives he of the wine-cup bright.
Him he hates, who day and night,
Gentle night and gladsome day,
Cares not thus to wile away.

σοφὰν δ' ἀπέχειν πραπίδα φρένα τε
περισσῶν παρὰ φωτῶν.
τὸ πλῆθος ὅ τι τὸ φαυλότερον
ἐνόμισε χρῆταί τε, τόδε τοι λέγοιμ ἄν.

BACCHÆ.

862—911.

ἆρ' ἐν παννυχίοις χοροῖς   στρ.
θήσω ποτὲ λευκὸν
πόδ' ἀναβακχεύουσα δέραν
   εἰς αἰθέρα δροσερὸν
ῥίπτουσ', ὡς νεβρὸς χλοεραῖς
ἐμπαίζουσα λείμακος ἡδοναῖς
ἡνίκ' ἂν φοβερὸν φύγῃ
θήραμ' ἔξω φυλακᾶς
εὐπλέκτων ὑπὲρ ἀρκύων,
θωΰσσων δὲ κυναγέτας
συντείνῃ δρόμημα κυνῶν,   ·
μόχθοις τ' ὠκυδρόμοις τ' ἀέλ-
λαις θρώσκῃ πεδίον
παραποτάμιον, ἡδομένα
βροτῶν ἐρημίαις,
σκιαροκόμου τ' ἐν ἔρνεσιν ὕλας.
τί τὸ σοφὸν ἢ τί τὸ κάλλιον
παρὰ θεῶν γέρας ἐν βροτοῖς
ἢ χεῖρ' ὑπὲρ κορυφᾶς
τῶν ἐχθρῶν κρείσσω κατέχειν;
ὅ τι καλὸν φίλον ἀεί.

Be thou wisely unsevere!
Shun the stern and the austere!
    Follow the multitude,
      Their usage still pursue;
        Their homely wisdom rude
    (Such is my sentence) is both right and true.

                    DEAN MILMAN.

BACCHÆ.

862—911.

O WHEN, through the long night
  With fleet foot glancing white,
Shall I go dancing in my revelry,
    My neck cast back, and bare
    Unto the dewy air,
Like sportive fawn in the green meadow's glee?
    Lo, in her fear she springs
    Over th' encircling rings,
Over the well-woven nets far off and fast;
    While swift along her track
    The huntsman cheers his pack,
With panting toil, and fiery storm-wind haste.
Where down the river-bank spreads the wide meadow,
    Rejoices she in the untrod solitude;
Couches at length beneath the silent shadow
    Of the old hospitable wood.

    What is wisest, what is fairest,
    Of God's boons to man the rarest?
    With the conscious conquering hand
    Above the foeman's head to stand.
    What is fairest still is dearest.

ὁρμᾶται μόλις, ἀλλ' ὅμως   ἀντ.
πιστὸν τό ϝε θεῖον
σθένος· ἀπευθεύνει δὲ βροτῶν
τούς τ' ἀϝνωμοσύναν
τιμῶντας καὶ μὴ τὰ θεῶν
αὔξοντας σὺν μαινομένᾳ δόξᾳ.
κρυπτεύουσι δὲ ποικίλως
δαρὸν χρόνου πύδα καὶ
θηρῶσιν τὸν ἄσεπτον. οὐ
ϝὰρ κρεῖσϑόν ποτε τῶν νόμων
ϝιϝνώσκειν χρὴ καὶ μελετᾶν.
κούφα ϝὰρ δαπάνα νομί-
ζειν ἰϑχὺν τόδ' ἔχειν,
ὅ τι ποτ' ἄρα τὸ δαιμόνιον,
τό τ' ἐν χρόνῳ μακρῷ
νόμιμον ἀεὶ φύσει τε πεφυκός.
τί τὸ σοφὸν ἢ τί τὸ κάλλιον
παρὰ θεῶν ϝέρας ἐν βροτοῖς
ἢ χεῖρ' ὑπὲρ κορυφᾶς
τῶν ἐχθρῶν κρείσϑω κατέχειν;
ὅ τι καλὸν φίλον ἀεί.

εὐδαίμων μὲν ὃς ἐκ θαλάϑϑας
ἔφυϝε κῦμα, λιμένα δ' ἔκιχεν·
εὐδαίμων δ' ὃς ὕπερθε μόχθων
ἐϝένεθ'· ἕτερα δ' ἕτεϝος ἕτερον
ὄλβῳ καὶ δυνάμει παρῆλθεν.
μυρίαι δὲ μυρίοισιν
ἔτ' εἶϑ' ἐλπίϲες· αἱ μὲν
τελευτῶσιν ἐν ὄλβῳ
βροτοῖς, αἱ δ' ἀπέβησαν·
τὸ δὲ κατ' ἦμαρ ὕτῳ βίοτος
εὐδαίμων, μακαρίζω.

Slow come, but come at length,
In their majestic strength,
Faithful and true, the avenging deities :
And chastening human folly,
And the mad pride unholy,
Of those who to the Gods bow not their knees.
For hidden still and mute
As glides their printless foot,
The impious on their winding path they hound.
For it is ill to know,
And it is ill to do,
Beyond the law's inexorable bound.
'Tis but light cost in his own power sublime
To array the Godhead, whosoe'er he be ;
And Law is old, even as the oldest time,
Nature's own unrepealed decree.

What is wisest, what is fairest,
Of God's boons to man the rarest ?
With the conscious conquering hand
Above the foeman's head to stand.
What is fairest still is rarest.

Who hath 'scaped the turbulent sea
And reached the haven, happy he !
Happy he whose toils are o'er,
In the race of wealth and power !
This one here and that one there
Passes by, and everywhere
Still expectant thousands over
Thousand hopes are seen to hover,
Some to mortals end in bliss ;
    Some have already fled away :
Happiness alone is his
    That happy is to-day.

DEAN MILMAN.

I 2

HECUBA.

444—483.

αὔρα, ποντιὰς αὔρα,   στρ. α΄.
ἅτε πυντοπόρους κομίζεις
θοὰς ἀκάτους ἐπ᾽ οἶδμα λίμνας,
ποῖ με τὰν μελέαν πορεύσεις;
τῷ δουλόσυνος πρὸς οἶκον
κτηθεῖσ᾽ ἀφίξομαι;
ἢ Δωρίδος ὅρμον αἴας,
ἢ Φθιάδος, ἔνθα καλλί-
στων ὑδάτων πατέρα
φασὶν Ἀπιδανὸν γύας λιπαίνειν;

ἢ νάσων, ἁλιήρει   ἀντ. α΄.
κώπᾳ πεμπομέναν τάλαιναν,
οἰκτρὰν βιοτὰν ἔχουσαν οἴκοις,
ἔνθα πρωτόγονός τε φοῖνιξ
δάφνα θ᾽ ἱεροὺς ἀνέσχε
πτόρθους Λατοῖ φίλα
ὠδῖνος ἄγαλμα δίας;
σὺν Δηλιάσιν τε κούραις
Ἀρτέμιδός τε θεᾶς
χρυσέαν ἄμπυκα τόξα τ᾽ εὐλογήσω;

ἢ Παλλάδος ἐν πόλει   στρ. β΄.
τᾶς καλλιδίφρου Ἀθα-
ναίας ἐν κροκέῳ πέπλῳ
ζεύξομαι ἄρματι πώλους, ἐν
δαιδαλταῖσι ποικίλλουσ᾽
ἀνθοκρόκοισι πήναις,
ἢ Τιτάνων γενεὰν,
τὰν Ζεὺς ἀμφιπύρῳ
κοιμίζει φλογμῷ Κρονίδας;

HECUBA.

444—483.

BREEZE, breeze of the sea,
    Who the wave-passers bearest home
    Swift and unwearied o'er the billows' foam,
Ah ! whither lead'st thou me
    Grief-worn ? whose house must have
    This thing—a captured slave ?

Or shall I reach a harbour strand
    Dorian or Phthian, where they tell
Apidanos o'erstreams the land,
    Father of fairest founts that well ?

Or else some island shore,
Urged, wretched, on my way with brine-splashed oar,
    To lead a life of weary sorrow there,
Where the first palm bare fruit,
Where the bay raised each sacred shoot
    To form a bower,
    Leto's protection in her trial hour ?

Or shall I, like Delian maiden,
    Sing of Artemis divine,
Golden filleted, bow-laden ?
    Or at Pallas' sacred shrine
The steeds to her fair chariot yoke
To bear her, clad in saffron cloke,
    And braid the silken garments thin
    With saffron flow'rets woven in ?

Or shall I sing the Titan brood,
    Whom Zeus, great Kronos' son,
    Poured twice-forged fire upon,
And did to lasting sleep by that fell bolt and rude ?

ὤμοι τεκέων ἐμῶν,   ἀντ. β'.
ὤμοι πατέρων, χθονός θ',
ἃ καπνῷ κατερείπεται
τυφομένα, δορίληπτος
πρὸς Ἀργείων· ἐγὼ δ' ἐν ξεί-
να χθονὶ δὴ κέκλημαι
δούλα, λιπυῦσ' Ἀσίαν
Εὐρώπας θεράπναν,
ἀλλάξασ' Ἅιδα θαλάμους.

HECUBA.

905—952.

σὺ μὲν, ὦ πατρὶς Ἰλιὰς,   στρ. α'.
τῶν ἀπορθήτων πόλις οὐκέτι λέξει·
τοῖον Ἑλλάνων νέφος ἀμφί σε κρύπτει
δορὶ δὴ δορὶ πέρσαν.
ἀπὸ δὲ στεφάναν κέκαρσαι
πύργων, κατὰ δ' αἰθάλου
κηλῖδ' οἰκτροτάταν κέχρωσαι,
τάλαιν', οὐκέτι σ' ἐμβατεύσω.

μεσονύκτιος ὠλλύμαν,   ἀντ. α'.
ἦμος ἐκ δείπνων ὕπνος ἡδὺς ἐπ' ὄσσοις
κίδναται, μολπᾶν δ' ἄπο καὶ χοροποιῶν
θυσιᾶν καταπαύσας
πόσις ἐν θαλάμοις ἔκειτο,
ξυστὸν δ' ἐπὶ πασσάλῳ,
ναύταν οὐκέθ' ὁρῶν ὅμιλον
Τροίαν Ἰλιάδ' ἐμβεβῶτα.

Ah sorrow for the young,
For those whose life was long,
    For all the land,
A heap of smoking ruin,
Spear-pierced to her undoing
    By Argive hand !

And I shall be a slave
    Within a country not my own,
      Leaving the land that Europe has o'erthrown.
'Scaping the chambers of the grave.

C. KEGAN PAUL.

HECUBA.

905—952.

THOU, then, O natal Troy ! no more
The city of the unsack'd shalt be,
So thick from dark Achaia's shore
The cloud of war hath covered thee.
    Ah ! not again I tread thy plain—
The spear—the spear hath rent thy pride,
The flame hath scarr'd thee deep and wide ;
    Thy coronal of towers is shorn,
And thou most piteous art—most naked and forlorn !

    I perish'd at the noon of night !
When sleep had seal'd each weary eye ;
    When the dance was o'er, and harps no more
Rang out in choral minstrelsy.
    In the dear bower of delight
      My husband slept in joy ;
        His shield and spear suspended near,
Secure he slept : that sailor band
Full sure he deem'd no more should stand
    Beneath the walls of Troy.

ἐγὼ δὲ πλόκαμον ἀναδέτοις   στρ. β'.
μίτραισιν ἐρρυθμιζόμαν
χρυσέων ἐνόπτρων
λεύσσουσ' ἀτέρμονας εἰς αὐγὰς,
ἐπιδέμνιος ὡς πέσοιμ' ἐς εὐνάν.
ἀνὰ δὲ κέλαδος ἔμολε πόλιν·
κέλευσμα δ' ἦν κατ' ἄστυ Τροίας τόδ'· ὦ
παῖδες Ἑλλάνων, πότε δὴ πότε τὰν
Ἰλιάδα σκοπιὰν
πέρσαντες ἥξετ' οἴκους;

λέχη δὲ φίλια μονόπεπλος   ἀντ. β'.
λιποῦσα, Δωρὶς ὡς κόρα,
σεμνὰν προσίζουσ'
οὐκ ἤνυσ' Ἄρτεμιν ἁ τλάμων·
ἄγομαι δὲ θανόντ' ἰδοῦσ' ἀκοίταν
τὸν ἐμὸν ἅλιον ἐπὶ πέλαγος,
πόλιν τ' ἀποσκοποῦσ', ἐπεὶ νόστιμον
ναῦς ἐκίνησεν πόδα καί μ' ἀπὸ γᾶς
ὥρισεν Ἰλιάδος·
τάλαιν', ἀπεῖπον ἄλγει·

τὰν τοῖν Διοσκόροιν Ἑλέναν κάσιν, Ἰ-   ἐπῳδ.
δαῖόν τε βούταν αἰνόπαριν κατάρᾳ
διδοῦσ', ἐπεί με γᾶς
ἐκ πατρίας ἀπώλεσεν
ἐξῴκισέν τ' οἴκων γάμος, οὐ γάμος, ἀλλ'
ἀλάστορός τις οἰζύς·
ἃν μήτε πέλαγος ἅλιον ἀπαγάγοι πάλιν,
μήτε πατρῷον ἵκοιτ' ἐς οἶκον.

And I too, by the taper's light,
  Which in the golden mirror's haze
  Flash'd its interminable rays,
Bound up the tresses of my hair,
That I Love's peaceful sleep might share.

I slept ; but, hark ! that war-shout dread,
Which rolling through the city spread ;
And this the cry,—" When, Sons of Greece,
When shall the lingering leaguer cease ?
When will ye spoil Troy's watch-tower high,
And home return ?"—I heard the cry,
And, starting from the genial bed,
Veiled, as a Doric maid, I fled,
And knelt, Diana, at thy holy fane,
A trembling suppliant—all in vain.

They led me to the sounding shore—
  Heavens ! as I passed the crowded way
  My bleeding lord before me lay—
I saw—I saw—and wept no more,
Till, as the homeward breezes bore
The bark returning o'er the sea,
My gaze, oh, Ilion, turn'd on thee !

Then, frantic, to the midnight air,
I cursed aloud the adulterous pair :
" They plunged me deep in exile's woe ;
They laid my country low :
  Their love—no love ! but some dark spell,
  In vengeance breath'd, by spirit fell.
Rise, hoary sea, in awful tide,
And whelm that vessel's guilty pride ;
Nor e'er, in high Mycenæ's hall,
Let Helen boast in peace of mighty Ilion's fall."

J. T. COLERIDGE.

IPHIGENEIA IN AULIDE.

1036—1097.

τίς ἄρ' ὑμέναιος διὰ λωτοῦ Λίβυος   στρ.
μετά τε φιλοχόρου κιθάρας
συρίγγων θ' ὑπὸ καλαμοεσ-
σᾶν ἔστασεν ἰακχάν,
ὅτ' ἀνὰ Πήλιον αἱ καλλιπλόκαμοι
Πιερίδες ἐν δαιτὶ θεῶν
χρυσεοσάνδαλον ἴχνος
ἐν ϝᾷ κρούουσαι
Πηλέως ἐς ϝάμον ἦλθον,
μελῳδοῖς Θέτιν ἀχήμασι τόν τ' Αἰακίδαν
Κενταύρων ἀν' ὄρος κλέουσαι
Πηλιάδα καθ' ὕλαν.
ὁ δὲ Δαρδανίδας, Διὸς
λέκτρων τρύφημα φίλον,
χρυσέοισιν ἄφυσσε λοιβὰν
ἐν κρατήρων ϝυάλοις,
ὁ Φρύϝιος Γανυμήδης.
παρὰ δὲ λευκοφαῆ
ψάμαθον εἰλισσύμεναι
κύκλια πεντήκοντα κόραι
Νηρέως ϝάμους ἐχόρευσαν.

ἀνὰ δ' ἐλάταισι στεφανώδει τε χλόᾳ   ἀντ.
θίασος ἔμολεν ἱπποβότας
Κενταύρων ἐπὶ δαῖτα τὰν
θεῶν κρατῆρά τε Βάκχου.
μέϝα δ' ἀνέκλαϝον, ὦ Νηρηὶ κύρα,
παῖδες Θεσσαλαί, μέϝα φῶς

IPHIGENEIA IN AULIDE.

1036—1097.

MERRILY rose the bridal strain,
With the pipe of reed, and the wild harp ringing,
With the Libyan flute, and the dancers' train,
    And the bright-haired Muses singing.

    On the turf elastic treading,
Up Pelion's steep with an airy bound
Their golden sandals they struck on the ground,
While the mighty Gods were feasting round,
    As they sped to Peleus' wedding.
  They left Pieria's fountain,
    On the leaf-crowned hill they stood,
    They breathed their softest, sweetest lays
    In the bride's and bridegroom's praise.
  Re-echoed the Centaurs' mountain,
    Re-echoed Pelion's wood.

The golden goblets crowned the Page,
    The Thunderer's darling boy,
In childhood's rosy age
    Snatched from the plains of Troy.
    Where on the silvery sand
      The noon-tide sun was glancing,
  The fifty Nereids, hand in hand,
    Were in giddy circles dancing.

The Centaurs' tramp rang up the hill,
    To feast with the Gods they trooped in haste,
    And at the board, by Bacchus graced,
The purpling bowl to fill.
    Grassy wreath and larch's bough
    Twined around each shaggy brow.

μάντις ὁ Φοῖβος ὁ Μουσᾶν τ'
εἰδὼς ϝεννάσεις,
Χείρων ἐξονόμηνεν,
ὃς ἥξει χθόνα λοϝχήρεσι σὺν Μυρμιδόνων
ἀσπισταῖς Πριάμοιο κλεινὰν
ϝαῖαν ἐκπυρώσων,
περὶ σώματι χρυσέων
ὅπλων Ἡφαιστοπόνων
κεκορυθμένος ἐνδύτ' ἐκ θεᾶς
ματρὸς δωρήματ' ἔχων
Θέτιδος, ἅ νιν ἔτικτε
μακάριον. τότε δαί-
μονες τᾶς εὐπάτριδος
ϝάμων Νηρῇδός τ' ἔθεσαν
πρώτας Πηλέως θ' ὑμεναίους.

σὲ δ' ἐπὶ κάρα στέψουσι καλλικόμαν
πλόκαμον Ἀρϝεῖοί, [ϝ' ἁλιᾶν]
ὥστε πετραίων ἀπ' ἄντρων
ἐλθοῦσαν [ὀρέων] μόσχον ἀκήρατον,
βρότειον αἱμάσσοντες λαιμόν·
οὐ σύριϝϝι τραφεῖσαν, οὐδ'
ἐν ῥοιβδήσεσι βουκόλων,
παρὰ δὲ μητέρι νυμφοκόμον
Ἰναχίδαις ϝάμον.
ποῦ τὸ τᾶς αἰδοῦς ἢ τὸ τᾶς
ἀρετᾶς δύνασιν ἔχει
σθένειν τι πρόσωπον;
ὑπότε τὸ μὲν ἄσεπτον ἔχει
δύναμιν, ἁ δ' ἀρετὰ κατόπι-
σθεν θνατοῖς ἀμελεῖται,
ἀνομία δὲ νόμων κρατεῖ,
καὶ μὴ κοινὸς ἀϝὼν βροτοῖς,
μή τις θεῶν φθόνος ἔλθῃ.

Daughter of Nereus, loud to thee
Chaunted the maids of Thessaly.
Their song was of a child unborn,
Whose light should beam like summer morn,
Whose praise by the Delian seer was sung,
And hymned by Chiron's tuneful tongue.

"Thetis, mark thy warrior son,
    Girt with many a Myrmidon,
    Armed with spear and flaming brand,
    Wasting Priam's ancient land.
    He shall ne'er to foeman quail;
    He shall case his limbs in mail,
    Casque, and greaves, and breast-plate's fold,
    All by Vulcan wrought of gold,
    Moulded in the forge of heaven,
    By his goddess-mother given.
    His shall be a hero's name,
    Godlike might, and deathless fame."

Thus the Gods propitious smiled
On Peleus and the ocean child ;
Lady ! not such nuptial wreath
    Shall Argives bid thee wear,
But with the flowers of death
    Entwine thy clustering hair.

J. ANSTICE.

CYCLOPS.

41—54.   68—81.

πᾶ δή μοι γενναίων μὲν πατέρων,   στρ.
γενναίων δ' ἐκ τοκάδων,
πᾶ δή μοι νίσσει σκοπέλους;
οὐ τᾷδ' ὑπήνεμος αὔρα
καὶ ποιηρὰ βοτάνα,
δινᾶέν θ' ὕδωρ ποταμῶν.
ἐν πίστραις κεῖται πέλας ἄντρων, οὖ σοι βλαχαὶ τεκέων.
ψύττ', οὐ τάδ' οὖν οὐ τάδε νεμεῖ,
οὐδ' αὖ κλιτὺν δροσεράν;
ὠή, ῥίψω πέτρον τάχα σου,
ὕπαγ' ὦ ὕπαγ' ὦ κεράστα
μηλοβότα στασίωρον *
Κύκλωπος ἀγροβότα.

*   *   *   *

Ἴακχον Ἴακχον ᾠδὰν
μέλπω πρὸς τὰν Ἀφροδίταν,
ἂν θηρεύων πετόμαν
Βάκχαις σὺν λευκόποσιν.
ὦ φίλος ὦ φίλε Βάκχιε,
ποῖ οἰοπολεῖς
ξανθὰν χαίταν σείων;
ἐγὼ δ' ὁ σὸς πρόσπολος
θητεύω Κύκλωπι
τῷ μονοδέρκτᾳ,
δοῦλος ἀλαίνων σὺν τᾷδε
τράγου χλαίνᾳ μελέᾳ
σᾶς χωρὶς φιλίας.

CYCLOPS.

41—54.   68—81.

WHERE has he of race divine
  Wandered in the winding rocks?
Here the air is calm and fine
  For the father of the flocks ;—
Here the grass is soft and sweet,
And the river-eddies meet
In the trough beside the cave,
Bright as in their fountain wave.—
Neither here, nor on the dew
  Of the lawny uplands feeding?
Oh, you come !—a stone at you
  Will I throw to mend your breeding ;—
Get along, you hornèd thing,
Wild, seditious, rambling !

*   *   *   *

An Iacchic melody
  To the golden Aphrodite
Will I lift, as erst did I
  Seeking her and her delight
With the Mænads, whose white feet
To the music glance and fleet.
Bacchus, O belovèd, where
Shaking wide thy yellow hair,
Wanderest thou alone, afar?
  To the one-eyed Cyclops we,
Who by right thy servants are,
  Minister in misery,
In these wretched goat-skins clad,
  Far from thy delights and thee.

P. B. SHELLEY.

CYCLOPS.

511—520.

καλὸν ὄμμασιν δεδορκώς
καλὸν ἐκπερᾷ μελάθρων.
* * φιλεῖ τις ἡμᾶς.
λύχνα δ᾽ ἡμμέν᾽ ἀμμένει σὸν
χρῶ᾽, ἄγ᾽ ὦ τέρεινα νύμφα
δροσερῶν ἔσωθεν ἄντρων.
στεφάνων δ᾽ οὐ μία χροιὰ
περὶ σὸν κρᾶτα τάχ᾽ ἐξομιλήσει.

CYCLOPS.

511—520.

ONE with eyes the fairest
  Cometh from his dwelling,
Some one loves thee, rarest,
  Bright beyond my telling.
In thy grace thou shinest
Like some nymph divinest,
In her caverns dewy :—
All delights pursue thee,
Soon pied flowers, sweet-breathing,
Shall thy head be wreathing.

P. B. SHELLEY.

ARISTOPHANES.

NUBES.

275—290.   298—313.

ἀέναοι Νεφέλαι,   στρ.
ἀρθῶμεν φανεραὶ δροσερὰν φύσιν εὐάγητον,
πατρὶς ἀπ' Ὠκεανοῦ βαρυαχέος
ὑψηλῶν ὀρέων κορυφὰς ἐπὶ
δενδροκόμους, ἵνα
τηλεφανεῖς σκοπιὰς ἀφορώμεθα,
καρποὺς τ' ἀρδομέναν ἱερὰν χθόνα,
καὶ ποταμῶν ζαθέων κελαδήματα,
καὶ πόντον κελάδοντα βαρύβρομον·
ὄμμα γὰρ αἰθέρος ἀκάματον σελαγεῖται
μαρμαρέαις ἐν αὐγαῖς.
ἀλλ' ἀποσεισάμεναι νέφος ὄμβριον
ἀθανάτας ἰδέας ἐπιδώμεθα
τηλεσκόπῳ ὄμματι γαῖαν.

*   *   *   *

παρθένοι ὀμβροφόροι,   ἀντ.
ἔλθωμεν λιπαρὰν χθόνα Παλλάδος, εὔανδρον γᾶν
Κέκροπος ὀψόμεναι πολυήρατον·
οὗ σέβας ἀρρήτων ἱερῶν, ἵνα
μυστοδόκος δόμος
ἐν τελεταῖς ἁγίαις ἀναδείκνυται,
οὐρανίοις τε θεοῖς δωρήματα,
ναοί θ' ὑψερεφεῖς καὶ ἀγάλματα,
καὶ πρόσοδοι μακάρων ἱερώταται,
εὐστέφανοί τε θεῶν θυσίαι θαλίαι τε,
παντοδαπαῖς ἐν ὥραις,

NUBES.

275—290.   298—313.

CLOUD-MAIDENS that float on for ever,
    Dew-sprinkled, fleet bodies, and fair,
Let us rise from our Sire's loud river,
    Great Ocean, and soar through the air
To the peaks of the pine-covered mountains where the
    pines hang as tresses of hair.
Let us seek the watchtowers undaunted,
    Where the well-watered cornfields abound,
And through murmurs of rivers nymph-haunted
    The songs of the sea-waves resound ;
And the sun in the sky never wearies of spreading his
    radiance around.
            Let us cast off the haze
                Of the mists from our band,
            Till with far-seeing gaze
                We may look on the land.

*   *   *   *

Cloud-maidens that bring the rain-shower,
    To the Pallas-loved land let us wing,
To the land of stout heroes and Power,
    Where Kekrops was hero and king,
Where honour and silence is given
    To the mysteries that none may declare,
Where are gifts to the high gods in heaven
    When the house of the gods is laid bare,
Where are lofty roofed temples, and statues well
    carven and fair ;
Where are feasts to the happy immortals
When the sacred procession draws near,
    Where garlands make bright the bright portals
At all seasons and months in the year ;

ἦρί τ᾽ ἐπερχομένῳ Βρομία χάρις,
εὐκελάδων τε χορῶν ἐρεθίσματα,
καὶ Μοῦσα βαρύβρομος αὐλῶν.

AVES.

211—222.　　227—262.

ἅγε σύννομέ μοι, παῦσαι μὲν ὕπνου,
λῦσον δὲ νόμους ἱερῶν ὕμνων,
οὓς διὰ θείου στόματος θρηνεῖς,
τὸν ἐμὸν καὶ σὸν πολύδακρυν Ἴτυν
† ἐλελιζομένη διεροῖς μέλεσιν
γένυος ξουθῆς·
καθαρὰ χωρεῖ διὰ φυλλοκόμου
μίλακος ἠχὼ πρὸς Διὸς ἕδρας,
ἵν᾽ ὁ χρυσοκόμας Φοῖβος ἀκούων.
τοῖς σοῖς ἐλέγοις ἀντιψάλλων
ἐλεφαντόδετον φόρμιγγα, θεῶν
ἵστησι χορούς·
διὰ δ᾽ ἀθανάτων στομάτων χωρεῖ
ξύμφωνος ὁμοῦ
θεία μακάρων ὀλολυγή.
(αὐλεῖ.)

　　*　　　　*　　　　*　　　　*

ἐποποποποποποποποποποποί,
ἰὼ ἰώ, ἰτώ ἰτώ ἰτώ ἰτώ
ἴτω τις ὧδε τῶν ἐμῶν ὁμοπτέρων·
ὅσοι τ᾽ εὐσπόρους ἀγροίκων γύας
νέμεσθε, φῦλα μυρία κριθοτράγων
σπερμολόγων τε γένη
ταχὺ πετόμενα, μαλθακὴν ἱέντα γῆρυν·

And when spring days are here,
Then we tread to the wine-god a measure,
In Bacchanal dance and in pleasure,
'Mid the contests of sweet singing choirs,
And the crash of loud lyres.

OSCAR WILDE.

Oxford, 1874.

AVES.

211—222.   227—262.

CEASE, my mate, from slumber now ;
Let the sacred hymn-notes flow,
Wailing with thy voice divine
Long-wept Itys, mine and thine.
So, when thy brown beak is thrilling
With that holy music-trilling,
Through the woodbine's leafy bound
Swells the pure melodious sound
To the throne of Zeus : and there
Phœbus of the golden hair,
Hearing, to thine elegies
With awaken'd chords replies
Of his ivory-claspèd lyre,
Stirring all the Olympian quire ;
Till from each immortal tongue
Of that blessèd heavenly throng
Peals the full harmonious song.

*   *   *   *

Epopopopopopopopopopopoi !
Holloa! holloa ! What ho ! what ho !
Hither haste, my plume-partakers ;
Come many, come any
That pasture on the farmer's well-sown acres,
Tribes countless that on barley feed,
And clans that gather out the seed ;

ὅϲα τ᾽ ἐν ἄλοκι θαμὰ
βῶλον ἀμφιτιττυβίζεθ᾽ ὧδε λεπτὸν
ἡδομένᾳ φωνᾷ·
τιὸ τιὸ τιὸ τιὸ τιὸ τιὸ τιὸ τιό·
ὅϲα θ᾽ ὑμῶν κατὰ κήπους ἐπὶ κιϲϲοῦ
κλάδεϲι νομὸν ἔχει,
τά τε κατ᾽ ὄρεα, τά τε κοτινοτράγα, τά τε κομαροφάγα,
ἀνύϲατε πετόμενα πρὸς ἐμὰν ἀοιδάν·
τριοτὸ τριοτὸ τοτοβρίξ·
οἵ θ᾽ ἑλείας παρ᾽ αὐλῶνας ἰευϲτόμους
ἐμπίδας κάπτεθ᾽, ὅϲα τ᾽ εὐδρόϲους γῆς τόπους
ἔχετε λειμῶνά τ᾽ ἐρόεντα Μαραθῶνος,
ὄρνις τε πτεροποίκιλος
ἀτταγᾶς ἀτταγᾶς.
ὧν τ᾽ ἐπὶ πόντιον οἶδμα θαλάϲϲης
φῦλα μετ᾽ ἀλκυόνεϲϲι ποτᾶται,
δεῦρ᾽ ἴτε πευϲόμενοι τὰ νεώτερα,
πάντα γὰρ ἐνθάδε φῦλ᾽ ἀθροΐζομεν
οἰωνῶν ταναοδείρων.
ἥκει γάρ τις δριμὺς πρέϲβυς,
καινὸς γνώμην,
καινῶν ἔργων τ᾽ ἐγχειρητής.
ἀλλ᾽ ἴτ᾽ ἐς λόγους ἅπαντα,
δεῦρο δεῦρο δεῦρο δεῦρο.
τοροτοροτοροτοροτίξ.
κικκαβαῦ κικκαβαῦ.
τοροτοροτοροτοροτορολιλιλίξ.

Come, alert upon the wing,
Dulcet music uttering :
Ye that o'er the furrowed sod
Twitter upon every clod,
Making all the air rejoice
With your soft and slender voice :
Tio, tio, tio, tio, tio, tio, tio, tio.
Ye that feast on garden fruits,
Nestling midst the ivy shoots :
Ye that all the mountains throng,
Olive-croppers, arbute-loppers,
Haste and fly to greet my song.
Trioto, trioto, totobrix !
Ye that o'er the marshy flats
Swallow down the shrill-mouthed gnats ;
Ye that haunt the deep-dew'd ground
Marathon's sweet meads around,
Ouzel, and thou of the speckled wing,
Hazelhen, hazelhen, speed while I sing.
Come many, come any
With the halcyon brood that sweep
Surges of the watery deep,
Come and list to novel words,
Which to hear, from far and near
We gather all the tribes of neck-extending birds.
Here is arrived a sharp old man
Of revolutionary mind,
To revolutionary deeds inclined :
Come all, and listen to his plan.
Hither, hither, hither, hither,
Torotorotorotorotix.
Kikkabau, kikkabau,
Torotorotorotorolililix.

BENJAMIN HALL KENNEDY.

AVES.

685—722.

Ἄγε δὴ φύσιν ἄνδρες ἀμαυρόβιοι, φύλλων γενεᾷ προσόμοιοι,
ὀλιγοδρανέες, πλάσματα πηλοῦ, σκιοειδέα φῦλ᾽ ἀμενηνά,
ἀπτῆνες ἐφημέριοι ταλαοὶ βροτοί, ἀνέρες εἰκελόνειροι,
πρόσχετε τὸν νοῦν τοῖς ἀθανάτοις ἡμῖν, τοῖς αἰὲν ἐοῦσι,
τοῖς αἰθερίοις, τοῖσιν ἀγήρῳς, τοῖς ἄφθιτα μηδομένοισιν.
ἵν᾽ ἀκούσαντες πάντα παρ᾽ ἡμῶν ὀρθῶς περὶ τῶν μετεώρων,
φύσιν οἰωνῶν γένεσίν τε θεῶν ποταμῶν τ᾽ Ἐρέβους τε
     Χάους τε
εἰδότες ὀρθῶς παρ᾽ ἐμοῦ Προδίκῳ κλάειν εἴπητε τὸ λοιπόν.
Χάος ἦν καὶ Νὺξ Ἔρεβός τε μέλαν πρῶτον καὶ Τάρταρος
     εὐρύς·
γῆ δ᾽ οὐδ᾽ ἀὴρ οὐδ᾽ οὐρανὸς ἦν· Ἐρέβους δ᾽ ἐν ἀπείροσι
     κόλποις
τίκτει πρώτιστον ὑπηνέμιον Νὺξ ἡ μελανόπτερος ᾠόν,
ἐξ οὗ περιτελλομέναις ὥραις ἔβλαστεν Ἔρως ὁ ποθεινός,
στίλβων νῶτον πτερύγοιν χρυσαῖν, εἰκὼς ἀνεμώκεσι δίναις.
οὗτος δὲ Χάει πτερόεντι μιγεὶς νυχίῳ κατὰ Τάρταρον εὐρὺν
ἐνεύττευσεν γένος ἡμέτερον, καὶ πρῶτον ἀνήγαγεν ἐς φῶς.

AVES.

685—722.

Come on then, ye dwellers by nature in darkness, and
  like to the leaves' generations
That are little of might, that are moulded of mire, un-
  enduring and shadowlike nations,
Poor plumeless ephemerals, comfortless mortals, as visions
  of creatures fast fleeing,
Lift up your mind unto us that are deathless, and dateless
  the date of our being :
Us, children of heaven, us, ageless for aye, us, all of
  whose thoughts are eternal ;
That ye may from henceforth, having heard of us all
  things aright as to matters supernal,
Of the being of birds and beginning of gods, and of
  streams, and the dark beyond reaching,
Truthfully knowing aright, in my name bid Prodicus pack
  with his preaching.

It was Chaos and Night at the first, and the blackness of
  darkness, and hell's broad border,
Earth was not, nor air, neither heaven ; when in depths
  of the womb of the dark without order
First thing first-born of the black-plumed Night was a
  wind-egg hatched in her bosom,
Whence timely with seasons revolving again sweet Love
  burst out as a blossom,
Gold wings glittering forth of his back, like whirlwinds
  gustily turning.
He, after his wedlock with Chaos, whose wings are of
  darkness, in hell broad-burning,
For his nestlings begat him the race of us first and
  upraised us to light new-lighted.

πρότερον δ' οὐκ ἦν γένος ἀθανάτων, πρὶν Ἔρως ξυνέμιξεν
   ἅπαντα·
ξυμμιγνυμένων δ' ἑτέρων ἑτέροις γένετ' οὐρανὸς ὠκεανός τε
καὶ γῆ πάντων τε θεῶν μακάρων γένος ἄφθιτον. ὧδε μέν
   ἐσμέν
πολὺ πρεσβύτατοι πάντων μακάρων. ἡμεῖς δ' ὡς ἐσμέν
   Ἔρωτος
πολλοῖς δῆλον· πετόμεσθά τε γὰρ καὶ τοῖσιν ἐρῶσι σύνεσμεν·
πολλοὺς δὲ καλοὺς ἀπομωμοκότας παῖδας πρὸς τέρμασιν
   ὥρας
διὰ τὴν ἰσχὺν τὴν ἡμετέραν διεμήρισαν ἄνδρες ἐρασταί,
ὁ μὲν ὄρτυγα δούς, ὁ δὲ πορφυρίων', ὁ δὲ χῆν', ὁ δὲ Περσικὸν
   ὄρνιν.
πάντα δὲ θνητοῖς ἐστὶν ἀφ' ἡμῶν τῶν ὀρνίθων τὰ μέγιστα.
πρῶτα μὲν ὥρας φαίνομεν ἡμεῖς ἦρος, χειμῶνος, ὀπώρας·
σπείρειν μέν, ὅταν γέρανος κρώζουσ' ἐς τὴν Λιβύην μεταχωρῇ,
καὶ πηδάλιον τότε ναυκλήρῳ φράζει κρεμάσαντι καθεύδειν,
εἶτα δ' Ὀρέστῃ χλαῖναν ὑφαίνειν, ἵνα μὴ ῥιγῶν ἀποδύῃ.
ἰκτῖνος δ' αὖ μετὰ ταῦτα φανεὶς ἑτέραν ὥραν ἀποφαίνει,
ἡνίκα πεκτεῖν ὥρα προβάτων πόκον ἠρινόν· εἶτα χελιδών,
ὅτε χρὴ χλαῖναν πωλεῖν ἤδη καὶ ληδάριόν τι πρίασθαι.
ἐσμὲν δ' ὑμῖν Ἄμμων, Δελφοί, Δωδώνη, Φοῖβος Ἀπόλλων.

And before this was not the race of the gods, until all
    things by Love were united ;
And of kind united with kind in communion of nature the
    sky and the sea are
Brought forth, and the earth, and the race of the gods
    everlasting and blest. So that we are
Far away the most ancient of all things blest. And that
    we are of Love's generation
There are manifest manifold signs. We have wings, and
    with us have the Loves habitation ;
And manifold fair young folk that forswore love once, ere
    the bloom of them ended,
Have the men that pursued and desired them subdued,
    by the help of us only befriended,
With such baits as a quail, a flamingo, a goose, or a
    cock's comb staring and splendid.

All best good things that befall men come from us birds,
    as is plain to all reason :
For first we proclaim and make known to them spring,
    and the winter and autumn in season ;
Bid sow, when the crane starts clanging for Afric, in
    shrill-voiced emigrant number.
And calls to the pilot to hang up his rudder again for the
    season, and slumber ;
And then weave a cloak for Prestes the thief, lest he
    strip men of theirs if it freezes.
And again thereafter the kite reappearing announces a
    change in the breezes,
And that here is the season for shearing your sheep of
    their spring wool. Then does the swallow
Give you notice to sell your greatcoat, and provide some-
    thing light for the heat that's to follow.
Thus are we as Ammon or Delphi unto you, Dodona, nay,
    Phœbus Apollo,

ἐλθόντες γὰρ πρῶτον ἐπ' ὄρνις, οὕτω πρὸς ἅπαντα τρέπεσθε,
πρός τ' ἐμπορίαν καὶ πρὸς βιότου κτῆσιν καὶ πρὸς γάμον
    ἀνδρός·
ὄρνιν τε νομίζετε πάνθ' ὅσαπερ περὶ μαντείας διακρίνει·
φήμη γ' ὑμῖν ὄρνις ἐστί, πταρμόν τ' ὄρνιθα καλεῖτε,
ξύμβολον ὄρνιν, φωνὴν ὄρνιν, θεράποντ' ὄρνιν, ὄνον ὄρνιν.
ἆρ' οὐ φανερῶς ἡμεῖς ὑμῖν ἐσμὲν μαντεῖος Ἀπόλλων;

AVES.

737—752.   769—783.

Μοῦσα λοχμαία,   στρ.
τιὸ τιὸ τιὸ τιὸ τιὸ τιὸ τιοτίγξ,
ποικίλη, μεθ' ἧς ἐγὼ
νάπαισι καὶ κορυφαῖς ἐν ὀρείαις,
τιὸ τιὸ τιὸ τιοτίγξ,
ἱζόμενος μελίας ἐπὶ φυλλοκόμου,
τιὸ τιὸ τιὸ τιοτίγξ,
δι' ἐμῆς γένυος ξουθῆς μελέων
Πανὶ νόμους ἱεροὺς ἀναφαίνω
σεμνά τε μητρὶ χορεύματ' ὑρεία,
τοτοτοτοτοτοτοτοτοτίγξ,
ἔνθεν ὡσπερεὶ μέλιττα
Φρύνιχος ἀμβροσίων μελέων ἀπεβόσκετο καρπόν, ἀεὶ φέ-
ρων γλυκεῖαν ᾠδάν.
τιὸ τιὸ τιὸ τιοτίγξ.

        *   *   *   *

For, as first ye come all to get auguries of birds, even
    such is in all things your carriage,
Be the matter a matter of trade, or of earning your bread,
    or of any one's marriage ;
And all things ye lay to the charge of a bird that belong
    to discerning prediction :
Winged fame is a bird, as you reckon : you sneeze, and
    the sign's as a bird for conviction :
All tokens are "birds" with you—sounds too, and lackeys,
    and donkeys.   Then must it not follow
That we ARE to you all as the manifold godhead that
    speaks in prophetic Apollo?

A. C. SWINBURNE.

AVES.

737—752.   769—783.

MUSE, that in the deep recesses
    Of the forest's dreary shade,
Vocal with our wild addresses ;
    Or in the lonely lowly glade,
Attending near, art pleased to hear
    Our humble bill tuneful and shrill.

When, to the name of omnipotent Pan,
    Our notes we raise, or sing in praise,
Of mighty Cybelè, from whom we began ;
    Mother of Nature, and every creature,
Winged or unwingèd, of birds or man.
    Aid and attend, and chant with me
The music of Phrynichus, open and plain,
    The first that attempted a loftier strain,
Ever busy like the bee, with the sweets of harmony.

   *   *   *   *

τοιάδε, κύκνοι,　　　　　　　　　　　　　　　　　　　ἀντ.
τιὸ τιὸ τιὸ τιὸ τιὸ τιὸ τιοτίγξ,
συμμιγῆ βοὴν ὁμοῦ
πτεροῖς κρέκοντες ἴαχον Ἀπόλλω,
τιὸ τιὸ τιὸ τιοτίγξ,
ὄχθῳ ἐφεζόμενοι παρ' Ἑβρον ποταμὸν,
τιὸ τιὸ τιὸ τιοτίγξ,
διὰ δ' αἰθέριον νέφος ἦλθε βοά·
πτῆξε δὲ ποικίλα φῦλά τε θηρῶν,
κύματά τ' ἔσβεσε νήνεμος αἴθρη,
τοτοτοτοτοτοτοτοτοτίγξ·
πᾶς δ' ἐπεκτύπησ' Ὄλυμπος·
εἷλε δὲ θάμβος ἄνακτας· Ὀλυμπιάδες δὲ μέλος Χάριτες
　　Μοῦ-
σαί τ' ἐπωλόλυξαν.
τιὸ τιὸ τιὸ τιοτίγξ.

RANÆ.

324—336.　　340—352.

Ἴακχ', ὦ πολυτίμητ' ἐν ἕδραις ἐνθάδε ναίων,　　　　στρ.
Ἴακχ', ὦ Ἴακχε,
ἐλθὲ τόνδ' ἀνὰ λειμῶνα χορεύσων,
ὁσίους ἐς θιασώτας,
πολύκαρπον μὲν τινάσσων
περὶ κρατὶ σῷ βρύοντα

Thus the swans in chorus follow,
  On the mighty Thracian stream,
  Hymning their eternal theme,
Praise to Bacchus and Apollo :
  The welkin rings, with sounding wings,
  With songs and cries and melodies :
  Up to the thunderous Æther ascending :

  Whilst all that breathe on earth beneath,
  The beasts of the wood, the plain and the flood,
In panic amazement are crouching and bending
    With the awful qualm of a sudden calm,
Ocean and air in silence blending.
The ridge of Olympus is sounding on high,
Appalling with wonder the lords of the sky,
    And the Muses and Graces,
    Enthroned in their places,
Join in the solemn symphony.

JOHN HOOKHAM FRERE.

RANÆ.

324—336.   340—352.

MIGHTY Bacchus !   Holy Power !
Hither at the wonted hour
    Come away,
    Come away,
  With the wanton holiday,
Where the revel uproar leads
To the mystic holy meads,
Where the frolic votaries fly,
With a tipsy shout and cry ;

στέφανον μύρτων· θρασεῖ δ' ἐγκατακρούων
ποδὶ τὰν ἀκόλαστον
φιλοπαίγμονα τιμάν,
χαρίτων πλεῖστον ἔχουσαν μέρος, ἁγνάν, ἱερὰν
ὁσίοις μύσταις χορείαν.

*   *   *   *

ἔγειρε φλογέας λαμπάδας ἐν χερσὶ τινάσσων,   ἀντ.
Ἴακχ', ὦ Ἴακχε,
νυκτέρου τελετῆς φωσφόρος ἀστήρ.
φλογὶ φέγγεται δὲ λειμών·
γόνυ πάλλεται γερόντων·
ἀποσείονται δὲ λύπας
χρονίους τ' ἐτῶν παλαιῶν ἐνιαυτούς,
ἱερᾶς ὑπὸ τιμᾶς.
σὺ δὲ λαμπάδι φέγγων
προβάδην ἔξαγ' ἐπ' ἀνθηρὸν ἕλειον δάπεδον
χοροποιὸν, μάκαρ, ἥβαν.

Flourishing the Thyrsus high,
Flinging forth, alert and airy,
To the sacred old vagary,
The tumultuous dance and song,
Sacred from the vulgar throng ;
Mystic orgies that are known
To the votaries alone—
To the mystic chorus solely—
Secret—unreveal'd—and holy.

*   *   *   *

Raise the fiery torches high !
Bacchus is approaching nigh,
Like the planet of the morn,
Breaking with the hoary dawn
    On the dark solemnity—
There they flash upon the sight ;
All the plain is blazing bright,
Flush'd and overflown with light.
Age has cast his years away,
And the cares of many a day,
Sporting to the lively lay—
Mighty Bacchus ! march and lead
(Torch in hand toward the mead)
Thy devoted humble chorus,
Mighty Bacchus,—move before us !

JOHN HOOKHAM FRERE.

NOTES.

PROMETHEUS.

398—434.

The chorus of Ocean Nymphs laments the cruel punishment of Prometheus for his rebellion against Zeus. In the last line of strophe i. Mrs. Browning adopted the reading ἐνδείκνυσιν for ἐν, δείκνυσιν.

528—559.

In default of any more adequate rendering of this chorus, Byron's paraphrase, written Dec. 1st, 1804, at Harrow, deserves quotation. Awed by Prometheus' punishment the Ocean nymphs express their submission to Zeus, and contrast his victim's present tortures with a happier scene.

Great Jove, to whose almighty throne
    Both gods and mortals homage pay,
Ne'er may my soul thy power disown,
    Thy dread behests ne'er disobey.
Oft shall the sacred victim fall
In sea-girt Ocean's mossy hall ;
My voice shall raise no impious strain
'Gainst him who rules the sky and azure main.

How different now thy joyless fate,
    Since first Hesionè thy bride,
When placed aloft in godlike state,
    The blushing beauty by thy side,
Thou sat'st, while reverend Ocean smiled,
And mirthful strains the hours beguiled ;
The Nymphs and Tritons danced around,
Nor yet thy doom was fix'd, nor Jove relentless frown'd.

887—906.

Io, the victim of the love of Zeus and the jealousy of Herè, has come upon the stage, and told the story of her sufferings. The Ocean Nymphs utter the eminently Greek prayer for an equal marriage. Compare the proverb attributed to Pittacus, τὴν κατὰ σαυτὸν ἔλα, with its implied meaning "Choose one of your own rank."

SEPTEM CONTRA THEBAS.

720—791.

Adrastus and Polyneices and the five other confederate chiefs have arrived against the walls of Thebes to do battle with Eteocles, the brother of Polyneices. The chorus of Theban maidens recites the history of the house, the marriage of Laius and Jocasta, the exposure of their child Œdipus, his return to Thebes and deliverance of the city from the Sphinx, his unwittingly incestuous marriage with his mother, the discovery that he was the slayer of his father, his blindness and exile, and the curse he launched against his sons, Eteocles and Polyneices, for their cruelty to him.

848—860.

Eteocles and Polyneices have slain each other in single combat. The Theban maidens lament them.

PERSÆ.

65—138.

The *Persæ* formed part of a trilogy with which Æschylus gained the prize in 472 B.C., only eight years after the Persian invasion and before peace had been concluded. In this chorus the Persian Elders from magnifying the splendour of the enormous army of Xerxes pass gradually to a strain of foreboding. In her translation Miss Swanwick adopted the text of Paley, which for the third line of the mesode reads :

φιλόφρων ͬὰρ ποτισαίνουσα τὸ πρῶτον παρ᾽ͬει βροτὸν
εἰς ἄρκυας ῎Ατα.

Minor differences are ἔσσεται for ἅσεται in the fourth anti-strophe, and ἁβροπενθεῖς for ἀκροπενθεῖς in the fifth.

SUPPLICES.

85—101.

Danaüs and Ægyptus were twin sons of Belus. The fifty sons of Ægyptus desired the fifty daughters of Danaüs in marriage, but the Danaides fled from them to Argos where they became Suppliants for the protection of Pelasgus, its king. The fragment here given from their opening chorus is expressive of their trust in Zeus. In the first line Professor Campbell reads εἶθ᾽ εἴн for εἰ θεἴн, and in the last but one ἄπονον δαιμονίαν instead of ἄποινον δαιμονίων.

AGAMEMNON.

105—257.

In this great chorus the Argive elders sing the sacrifice of Iphigeneia, the daughter of Agamemnon and Clytemnestra. Agamemnon had violated the sanctity of a grove of Artemis by killing in it a stag, and the goddess in her wrath caused a calm by which the Greek expedition against Troy was kept weather-bound at Aulis. At the instigation of the seer Calchas, Agamemnon, to appease the goddess, consented to sacrifice Iphigeneia, but at the moment of the sacrifice Artemis put a hart in her place and carried Iphigeneia herself to Tauris, there to act as her priestess. The chorus, alike from its beauty, its occasional obscurity, and its length, demands more from its translators than almost any other in Greek tragedy. Dean Milman's version is more evenly sustained throughout than any of its competitors with which I am acquainted. But the opening strophe and antistrophe are certainly better rendered by Conington in the following vigorous lines :

> I am the man !   I must be up and telling
>   The signs which met the chieftains on their way.
> I am the man—within me yet is swelling,
>   From heaven itself, the promptings of the lay,
>   The genial strength proportioned to my day—
>   How the chiefs of Greece in their twin-throned power,
>   The united crown of Achæa's flower,
>   There sends with spear and avenging hand
>   The imperial bird to the Trojan land,
>   The king of the fowls to the kings of the fleet—
>   One eagle black, one white on the back—
>   Appearing near on the hand of the spear
>   In the high-pitched pride of their stately seat :—
> They twain were devouring a hare and her brood,
> In the last of her courses borne down and subdued :
> Sing sorrow ! sing sorrow ! but triumph the good !
>
> Now as the wise host-prophet stood surveying
>   The two bold sons of Atreus, warriors true,
>   The fell devourers of the hare, portraying
>   Those missioned chieftains, all at once he knew,
>   And thus told out the signs that crossed his view :
>   " This journey of ours shall at length come down
>   In spoiler-wise upon Priam's town,
>   And the wealth of the people, the bulwark's store,
>   Shall Fate in her fury devour before.
>   Let but no grudge from the gods above
>   Cast envious might on the curb so bright,
>   For the queen of the chase abhors the race,
>   The winged hounds of her father Jove :—
>   For they ate a tame creature all quick with its brood :
>   The eagles she hates, and their banquet of blood :
>   Sing sorrow ! sing sorrow ! but triumph the good !"

In the fourth line of the first strophe Dean Milman apparently adopted the reading ἀλκάν.

160—183.

A fragment of this fragment first appeared in Mr. Myers' admirable essay on Æschylus in *Hellenica*. The translator kindly completed the passage for the present volume.

355—474.

The Argive Elders here sing of the punishment of Troy for its protection of Alexander (better known to us as Paris), after he had outraged the laws of hospitality by seducing Helen, the wife of his host Menelaus. The story of Helen's flight leads the chorus to sing her husband's sorrow, and from this they pass on to bewail the havoc caused by the long war.

In the celebrated crux in the second strophe, Mr. Morshead prefers the reading :

πάρεστι σῖγ', ἄτιμος ἀλλ' ἀλοίδορος,
ἄπιστος ἀφειμέναν ἰδών.

AGAMEMNON.

681—781.

The chorus here contrasts the joy and gaiety of Helen's arrival at Troy with the misery which her advent brought upon the city. The meaning of the first strophe rests on a play on Helen's name, which Prof. Campbell has wisely indicated instead of attempting to reproduce by a similar, but somewhat clumsy pun in English. "Hell of vessels, hell of heroes, hell of states," is Conington's rendering, while Dean Milman's

> "Helen call'd, the fated to destroy
> Ships and men and mighty Troy,"

preserves all the awkwardness of a pun with none of its point.

Prof. Campbell's variants in this chorus are rather numerous. They include κελσάντων for κέλσαντες in strophe i., and τίοντα (with suppression of comma after πρασσομένα) for τίοντος in the antistrophe ; λέοντος ἷνιν for λέοντα σίνιν

in strophe ii. ; and παρακλίνασ' for παρακλίνουσ' in strophe iii.
In the third line of strophe iv. φάος τόκου is adopted instead of
νεαρὰ φάους κότον, and the metre of the antistrophe is brought
into harmony with this by reading :

παλιντρόποις
ὕμμασι λιποῦσ', ὅσια προσέσυτο.

717—735.

The fragment here reprinted with Mr. Gladstone's permission
appeared in the volume of translations issued conjointly with
Lord Lyttelton in 1861, and reprinted in 1863. Its date of
composition is given as 1836.

In the antistrophe Mr. Gladstone reads :

ἔθος τὸ πρὸς τοκέων· χάριν
ϝὰρ τροφεῦσιν ἀμείβων.

CHOEPHOROE.

20—83.

Clytemnestra has slain Agamemnon, and at the opening of
this next act of the trilogy the chorus of captive Trojan women
are sent by her to bear offerings to her victim's grave.

This translation is extracted from a volume (for drawing my
attention to which I am greatly indebted to Mr. E. D. A.
Morshead) entitled, "Selections from the Choric Poetry of the
Greek Dramatic Writers, translated into English Verse, by
J. Anstice, B.A." (*London*, 1832, 8vo). According to the
Dictionary of National Biography, Mr. Joseph Anstice was born
in 1808, and educated at Westminster and Christ Church, Oxford,
where he wrote a prize poem on "Richard Cœur de Lion" and a
prize essay upon "The Influence of the Roman Conquests upon
Literature and the Arts in Rome." In 1831, when only 23, he
was appointed Professor of Classical Literature at King's College,
London, a post which four years later he was obliged by ill

health to resign. His death on Feb. 29th, 1836, at Torquay, cut short a career of singular promise. Of his translations I have already said something in my brief Introduction. The three specimens included in this volume will suffice to prove that, if sometimes lacking in conciseness and strength, they are characterized by a gracefulness and ease rarely found in translated work.

EUMENIDES.

307—396.

The murder of Agamemnon has been avenged, in accordance with the doom of the house, by his son, Orestes. The matricide is pursued by the avenging Furies, the Eumenides, who in this chorus sing of their appointed dues and functions. In his translation Dean Milman followed a text of the play, reading επι τόνως for ἐπὶ τὸν, ὦ, in the second strophe, and reversing the order of the last five lines of antistrophe ii. and strophe iii. His version, here reprinted by permission of Mr. Murray, appeared in the same volume which contains the Agamemnon and Bacchæ.

AJAX.

596—645.

Ajax, son of Telamon, king of Salamis, being worsted by Ulysses in the contention for the arms of Achilles, fell into a frenzy in which he slaughtered the sheep and oxen of the Greek host in the belief that they were his human enemies. The chorus of Salaminian sailors here imagine the misery that this ill news will cause when told in their island home.

693—718.

Ajax, awakened from his frenzy, recognizes that his mad acts have made life impossible, and goes forth to fall on his sword. But the Salaminian sailors mistake his object, and believing that all is well, and that they will soon sail homewards, sing and dance in an outburst of joy.

ŒDIPUS TYRANNUS.

151—215.

Laius, king of Thebes, was forewarned by an oracle that he should perish by the hand of his own son. To avert the fate, when Œdipus was born, his father caused him to be exposed on Mount Cithæron. The child was saved by a shepherd, and arrived at manhood without knowing his parentage. In a road-side quarrel he slew his father, Laius, and then proceeded to Thebes, where he delivered the city from the Sphinx, and obtained as his reward the kingdom and the hand of Jocasta, the widow of Laius, his own mother. In anger at this incestuous marriage and parricide the gods visited Thebes with a plague, and in this chorus the Theban Elders pray to heaven for mercy and relief from their woes.

Mr. Verrall writes with reference to his rendering, "As an excuse for the metrical liberties which have been made in this translation, it should perhaps be said, that it was not made independently, but to suit the music composed by Prof. Stanford for the original Greek, when the play was performed at Cambridge." The text adopted by the Greek Play Committee reads ἔνουρον and τελεῖν for ἄπουρον and τέλει in strophe iii., and προστιθέντα for προσταχθέντα in the antistrophe.

863—910.

Tiresias, the blind seer, has denounced Œdipus as the slayer of Laius. The king remembers the stranger whom he slew at the cross-roads, but there are some discrepancies in details, and in this pause of mingled hope and fear the Theban Elders sing this ode in praise of an innocent and humble life. In the second antistrophe they remember the ancient oracle as to the fate of Laius, and express their belief in it.

ŒDIPUS COLONEUS.

668—719.

Cast out from Thebes in accordance with his own decree, blinded by his own hands, Œdipus, attended only by his faithful daughter, Antigone, has come to Colonus, a suburb of Athens, there to find rest in death. He asks where he is, and the chorus of Elders of Colonus in telling him sing the praises of their village and of Attica. A legend tells us that at the end of his life, when nearly ninety, Sophocles established his sanity and capability of disposing of his own property, by reading to his judges this magnificent ode, then recently written. The play itself was not exhibited till 401 B.C., five years after the poet's death.

1211—1248.

His son, Polyneices, and his brother-in-law, Creon, torment the closing hours of the life of Œdipus. Theseus, prince of Athens, assures him of protection, and the chorus in sympathy sing of Death as the deliverer from all ills. The ode is perhaps the most beautiful in all Greek tragedy, and becomes the more impressive when we remember the great age which Sophocles had attained when he wrote it. In the works of Thomas Love Peacock there is a choral ode written in reminiscence of this, and he tells us that at one time Shelley was "always repeating" to himself the lines :

> Man's happiest lot is *not to be* :
> And when we tread life's thorny steep,
> Most blest are they, who, earliest free,
> Descend to death's eternal sleep,

though they lack the simplicity of the original.

In line 2 of strophe i., Mr. Housman reads παρὲκς for Dindorf's παρεὶς, and in line 10, δέοντος for θέλοντος. In the antistrophe he reverses the positions of φόνοι and φθόνος, and in the epode writes δ' ἐννυχιᾶν for δὲ νυχιᾶν.

ANTIGONE.

332—375.

The curse of Œdipus has fallen. His cruel sons, Eteocles and Polyneices have fought and slain each other, and now their uncle, Creon, is king, and has proclaimed that the body of Polyneices,

as the aggressor, is to be left unburied. A messenger announces
to Creon that his command has been disobeyed, and in this
chorus the Theban Elders sing the wonders of man in society,
and the necessity of obedience to law. A fine translation of this
Ode was made by Thomas Davidson, the Scottish Probationer.

583—625.

It is his sister, Antigone, who has buried Polyneices. She is
denounced to Creon, and condemned by him to death. The
Theban Elders sing the woes of the house of Œdipus, and the
divine anger by which it is pursued.

In the third and fourth lines of the second strophe, Mr.
Morshead reads :

ὁ παντ' ἀϝρεύων
οὔτε θεῶν ἄκματος,

and in the fifth ἀϝήρως for ἀϝήρῳ. The last two lines of the
same strophe he would print :

νόμος ὅδ' · οὐδὲν ἕρπει
θνατῶν βιότῳ πάμπολύ ϝ' ἐκτὸς ἄτας.

For his rendering of this chorus I wish to express my particular
obligations to Mr. Morshead, who, on my expressing my disap-
pointment at finding no version in existence which I quite liked,
very kindly made this translation, almost on the spur of the
moment, and placed it at my disposal.

781—800.

Hæmon, Creon's son, is Antigone's lover, and upbraids his
father for his cruel tyranny. Creon threatens to slay her before
his eyes, and Hæmon rushes from his presence. The chorus
then sings this short ode to Love.

In the last line but one, Sir G. Young reads with the MSS.
τῶν μεϝάλων πάρεδρος ἐν ἀρχαῖς θεσμῶν.

1115—1154.

The blind old seer, Tiresias, the same who had declared to
Œdipus his doom, has warned Creon of the fate to which his

cruelty is hastening him. Creon in terror orders the immediate release of Antigone from the rocky cell in which he has immured her, and the chorus breaks forth into this joyous prayer to Bacchus, the tutelary deity of Thebes. To the spectators, who knew the legend, their rejoicing must have sounded almost ironical, for Hæmon and Antigone have already done themselves to death.

MEDEA.

627—662.

Medea in her love for Jason not only saved his life, but abandoned her home at Colchis to follow him. He is now abandoning her for a Corinthian bride. The chorus of Corinthian women sings the danger of an overmastering love. In the first antistrophe Mr. Soutar (to whom I must apologize for omitting to place asterisks in the text) reads στέγοι for στέργοι, in the second strophe ὀικτρότατον for οἰκτροτάτων, in the antistrophe μῦθον for μύθων.

HIPPOLYTUS.

525—564.

Angered at the refusal of Hippolytus to yield her reverence, Aphrodite has smitten his step-mother, Phædra, with an unholy passion for him, against which she struggles in vain. The theme of this chorus, sung by Troizenian women, is closely similar to the one just quoted from the Medea. A translation by Thomas Love Peacock, not more beautiful than Madame Darmesteter's, but offering an interesting contrast of styles, will be found in the Appendix to Euripides.

ALCESTIS.

435—454.

Admetus in return for his hospitality to Apollo obtained from the Fates permission, at the time of his natural death, to substitute for himself his father, mother, or wife, if any one of these would consent to take his place. His wife, Alcestis, dies to save her husband, and the chorus of Pherœans thus bids her farewell. The translation is taken from the 1872 edition of the works of J. H. Frere, in which it appears as a fragment.

567—605.

At the moment of the death of Alcestis, Hercules comes to visit his friend Admetus. Fearing that if his guest were informed of his sorrow he would turn elsewhere, Admetus conceals his wife's death. The chorus praises his hospitable spirit, and call to mind the sojourn, in the house, of the god Apollo. The spirited version here quoted, first appeared in the pages of *Kottabos,* the magazine of Trinity College, Dublin, under the editorship of Prof. R. Y. Tyrrell.

962—1005.

When Hercules has learnt the truth as to his friend's sorrow, gratitude to Admetus sends him to struggle with Death, and wrest Alcestis from his grasp. While he is secretly gone on this errand Admetus laments for his wife, and the chorus sings this strain of consolation.

HELENA.

1451—1511.

According to the story adopted in this play, the Helen of the Trojan War was merely a wraith, the true Helen being all the time in Egypt, where she is discovered by Menelaus. The subject of this chorus is their return to Peloponnesus and to Sparta.

HERCULES FURENS.

348—441.

The last of the twelve labours of Hercules was his descent into the Lower World to fetch thence Cerberus and rescue his friend Theseus. While he was absent on this mission rumour reported his failure, and Lycus, King of Thebes, determined to destroy all his race, lest at any time they should avenge the murder of Creon. The chorus of Theban elders here celebrates the former exploits of Hercules, and laments the fate of his children and of his father Amphitryon, all of whom Lycus has condemned to death.

637—672.

Hercules has returned in safety in time to save his kinsfolk and punish Lycus. The chorus lament their old age, which has rendered them powerless when their help is needed. I quote in the Appendix to Euripides Peacock's version of this chorus, and may refer also to a spirited echo of it published in the *St. Andrews University Magazine, No. XI.*, by Mr. G. Soutar.

BACCHÆ.

370—431.

During the absence of Pentheus, King of Thebes, from his kingdom, the mystic worship of Bacchus has been introduced among his subjects. On his return he denounces it, and the chorus of Asiatic Bacchæ, by whom the worship of the god is being spread, here appeals to the goddess of Sanctity. Pentheus was subsequently driven mad by Bacchus, joined himself in woman's attire to the Bacchæ, and was torn to pieces by them.

862--911.

The song of the Bacchæ, whom Pentheus is about to join, as they proceed to the revels in which he is to meet his death. In the antistrophe they foreshadow his fate.

HECUBA.

444—483.

Troy has fallen, and Hecuba, its queen, and her daughter, Polyxena, are prisoners in the Greek camp. Polyxena had

been beloved by Achilles, and, according to one legend, his love
for her caused his doom. She is now to be sacrificed to his
shade, and this chorus is sung by the captive Trojan women, as
she goes to her death. The women, however, are occupied with
their own woes, and their song has nothing to do with
Polyxena.

905—952.

Fresh woes have fallen on Hecuba. The body of her son,
Polydorus, murdered by his guardian, Polymestor, has been
washed ashore, and she is now about to avenge the murder.
But the chorus are still mindful only of their own fate, and sing
this dirge over the fall of Troy. The first version here quoted
is taken from a footnote to the *Table Talk* of S. T. Coleridge.

IPHIGENEIA IN AULIDE.

1036—1097.

The subject of the *Iphigeneia in Aulis* is told in the closing
strophes of the first chorus of the Agamemnon. The chorus
here contrasts her fate with the gay scene at the marriage of
Peleus and Thetis. The relevance of their song is greatly
diminished in the spirited version of Mr. Anstice, by his unfortunate compression of the last eighteen lines into six.

CYLOPS.

41—54.　　68—81.

These stanzas form the strophe and epode of the chorus of
Satyrs in quest of their leader, Silenus. The antistrophe Shelley
omitted from his translation.

511—520.

A fragment from the song with which the chorus flatters the
drunken Cyclops.

NUBES.

275—290. 298—313.

The opening chorus of the Cloud-Maidens, as they float on the stage at the call of Socrates, whom Aristophanes represents as star-gazing from a basket swung in mid air.

AVES.

211—222. 227—262.

The call of the Hoopoe, bidding all the birds to a general assembly, does not come properly within the scope of this volume. But its lyric beauty and the pleasure of quoting the English version of Dr. Kennedy made its inclusion imperative. The translations by Frere and by Madame Darmesteter are both also noteworthy. In lines 212—215, Dr. Kennedy inserted a colon after Ἴτυν, and read ἐλελιζομένης δ' ἱεροῖς, with no stop after ἐουθῆς.

685—722.

The chorus of Birds give their theory of creation. Mr. Swinburne's magnificent version first appeared in the columns of the *Athenæum.*

737—752. 769—783.

"We see here a comic imitation of the tragic choruses of Phrynichus, a poet older than Æschylus, of whom Aristophanes always speaks with respect, as an improver of music and poetry."—*Frere's note.*

RANÆ.

324—336. 340—352.

A chorus of the Initiated in honour of Bacchus.

APPENDIX TO EURIPIDES.

PERMISSION to use Peacock's translations was not obtained till after the greater part of this volume was in type. I add them, therefore, in an Appendix, and join with them the less diffuse of Campbell's two versions from the Medea.

MEDEA.

HALLOWED earth, with indignation
　　Mark, oh mark, the murderous deed !
Radiant eye of wide creation,
　　Watch the damnèd parricide !

Yet, ere Colchis' rugged daughter
　　Perpetrate the dire design,
And consign to kindred slaughter
　　Children of thy golden line,

Shall the hand, with murder gory,
　　Cause immortal blood to flow !
Sun of heaven, arrayed in glory,
　　Rise—forbid—avert the blow !

In the vales of placid gladness
　　Let no rueful maniac range ;
Chase afar the Fiend of Madness,
　　Wrest the dagger from Revenge !

Say, hast thou, with kind protection
　　Reared thy smiling race in vain ;
Fostering Nature's fond affection,
　　Tender cares, and pleasing pain.

Hast thou on the troubled ocean
    Braved the tempest loud and strong,
Where the waves in wild commotion
    Roar Cyanean rocks among?

Didst thou roam the paths of danger,
    Hymenean joys to prove?
Spare, O sanguinary stranger,
    Pledges of thy sacred love!

Shall not Heaven, with indignation,
    Watch thee o'er the barbarous deed?
Shalt thou cleanse with expiation,
    Monstrous, murderous parricide?

THOMAS CAMPBELL.

HIPPOLYTUS.

525—564.

O LOVE ! O love ! whose shafts of fire
    Invade the soul with sweet surprise,
Through the soft dews of young desire
    Trembling in beauty's azure eyes !
Condemn not me the pangs to share
Thy too impassioned votaries bear,
That on the mind their stamp impress,
Indelible and measureless :
For not the sun's descending dart,
Nor yet the lightning brand of Jove,
Falls like the shaft that strikes the heart,
Thrown by the mightier hand of love.

Oh ! vainly, where, by Letrian plains,
    Tow'rd Dian's dome Alphëus bends,
And from Apollo's Pythian fanes,
    The steam of hecatombs ascends ;
While not to love our altars blaze ;
To love, whose tyrant power arrays
Against mankind each form of woe
That hopeless anguish bleeds to know :
To love who keeps the golden key,
    That, when more favoured lips implore,
Unlocks the sacred mystery
    Of youthful beauty's bridal door.

Alas ! round love's despotic power,
    Their brands what forms of terror wave !
The Œchalian maid in evil hour,
    Venus to greet Alcides gave.

As yet in passion's lore unread,
　　Unconscious of connubial ties,
She saw around her bridal bed
　　Her native city's flames arise.
All-hapless maid ! mid kindred gore
　　Whose nuptial torch the Furies bore !
To him consigned, an ill-starred bride,
　　By whom her sire and brethren died.

O towers of Thebes ! O sacred flow
　　Of mystic Dircè's fountain tides !
Say in what shapes of fear and woe
　　Love through his victim's bosom glides ?
She, who to heaven's imperial sire
　　The care-dispelling Bacchus bore,
'Mid thunder and celestial fire
　　Embraced, and slept, to wake no more.
Too powerful love, inspiring still　　　.
　　The dangerous risk, the frantic will,
Bears like the bee's mellifluous wing,
　　A transient sweet, a lasting sting.

THOMAS LOVE PEACOCK.

ALCESTIS.

962—1005.

My steps have pressed the flowers,
That to the Muses' bowers
The eternal dews of Helicon have given :
And trod the mountain height,
Where Science, young and bright,
Scans with poetic gaze the midnight-heaven ;
Yet have I found no power to vie
With thine, severe Necessity !
No counteracting spell sublime,
By Orpheus breathed in elder time,
The tablets of initiate Thrace contain :
No drug imbued with strength divine,
To sons of Æsculapian line
By pitying Phœbus taught, to soothe the stings of pain.

Thee, goddess, thee alone
None seek with suppliant moan :
No votive wreaths thine iron altars dress ;
Immutably severe,
The song thou dost not hear,
That speaks the plaint of mortal wretchedness.
Oh, may I ne'er more keenly feel
Thy power, that breaks the strength of steel,
With whose dread course concordant still
Jove executes his sovereign will :
Vain were his might, unseconded by thee.
Regret or shame thou canst not know ;
Nor pity for terrestrial woe
Can check thy onward course, or change thy stern decree.

And thou in patience bear thy doom,
Beneath her heaviest bonds opprest :
Tears cannot burst the marble tomb,
Where e'en the sons of gods must rest.
In life, in death, most loved, most blest,
Was she for whom our fruitless tears are shed ;
And round her cold sepulchral bed,
Unlike the tombs of the promiscuous dead,
Wreaths of eternal fame shall spread,
By matchless virtue merited.
There oft the traveller from his path shall turn,
And muse beneath the lonely cypress shade,
That waves, in silent gloom, where her remains are laid.

THOMAS LOVE PEACOCK.

HERCULES FURENS.

637—672.

To me the hours of youth of youth are dear,
In transient light that flow :
But age is heavy, cold and drear,
As winter's rocks of snow.
Already on my brows I feel
His grasp of ice and fangs of steel,
Dimming the visual radiance pale,
That soon eternal night shall veil.
Oh ! not for all the gold that flings,
Through domes of Oriental kings,
Its mingled splendour, falsely bright,
Would I resign youth's lovelier light.
For whether wealth its path illume,
Or toil and poverty depress,
The days of youth are days of bloom
And health and hope and loveliness.
Oh ! were the ruthless demon, Age,
Involved by Jove's tempestuous rage,
And fast and far to ruin driven,
Beyond the flaming bounds of heaven,
Or whelmed where arctic winter broods
O'er Ocean's frozen solitudes,
So never more to haunt again
The cities and the homes of men,—
Yet, were the gods the friends of worth,
Of justice and of truth,
The virtuous and the wise on earth
Should find a second youth.
Then would true glory shine unfurled,
A light to guide and guard the world,

If, not in vain with time at strife,
The good twice ran the race of life,
While vice, to one brief course confined,
Should wake no more to curse mankind.
Experience then might rightly trace
The lines that part the good and base,
As sailors read the stars of night,
Where shoreless billows murmuring roll,
And guide by their unerring light
The vessel to its distant goal.
But, since no signs from Jove declare
That earthly virtue claims his care ;
Since folly, vice and falsehood prove
As many marks of heavenly love ;
The life of man in darkness flies ;
The thirst of truth and wisdom dies ;
And love and beauty bow the knee
To gold's supreme divinity.

THOMAS LOVE PEACOCK.

A BIBLIOGRAPHY OF TRANSLATIONS

OF THE

GREEK DRAMATISTS INTO ENGLISH VERSE

N

ÆSCHYLUS.

The Tragedies of Æschylus; translated by Robert Potter. *Norwich*, 1777. 4⁰.

The date in the dedication of the "Notes" is July 11, 1778.

A second edition, "corrected," was published in London in 1779, 8⁰, and other editions followed in 1808, 1809, 1819, and 1833.

The Lyrical Dramas of Æschylus from the Greek; translated into English verse by J. S. Blackie.
London, 1850. 8⁰.

The Tragedies of Æschylos. A new translation, with a biographical essay, and an appendix of rhymed choral odes by E. H. Plumptre. 2 vols.
London, 1868. 8⁰.

A "second edition, revised," was published in 1873.

The Dramas of Æschylus; translated by A. Swanwick; with illustrations from Flaxman's designs.
London, 1873. fol.

A third edition was published in 1881 (8⁰) as part of Bohn's Classical Library.

The Agamemnon, Choephori, and Eumenides of Æschylus: translated into English verse by Anna Swanwick.
London, 1865. 8⁰.

An instalment of the complete edition published in 1873.

The Orestea of Æschylus; translated into English verse by C. N. Dalton, B.A.
London, 1868. 8⁰.

The House of Atreus: being the Agamemnon, Libation-Bearers, and Furies of Æschylus; translated into English verse by E. D. A. Morshead.
London, 1881. 8⁰.

A second edition was published in 1889.

The Agamemnon of Æschylus ; translated by Hugh Stuart Boyd.
London, 1823. 8⁰.

The Agamemnon of Æschylus ; translated by John Symmons.
London, 1824. 8".

The Agamemnon of Æschylus ; translated from the Greek ; illustrated by a dissertation on Grecian tragedy, &c., by J. S. Harford.
London, 1831. 8⁰.

Agamemnon : a tragedy from the Greek of Æschylus ; translated into English verse by Thomas Medwin.
London, 1832. 8⁰.

The Prometheus and Agamemnon ; translated from the Greek. *Part of The Death of Demosthenes, and other poems ; by George Croker Fox.*
London, 1839. 8⁰.

The Agamemnon of Æschylus ; translated literally and rhythmically by W. Sewell ; with a preface and notes.
London, 1846. 12⁰.

The Agamemnon ; the Greek text with a translation into English verse, and notes critical and explanatory ; by John Conington, B.A.
London, 1848. 8⁰.

Agamemnon the King ; a tragedy, from the Greek of Æschylus, by William Blew.
London, 1855. 8⁰.

The Agamemnon of Æschylus and the Bacchanals of Euripides ; with passages from the lyric and later poets of Greece, translated by Henry Hart Milman.
London, Edinburgh [printed], 1865. 8⁰.

The Agamemnon of Æschylus ; revised and translated by J. F. Davies. *Gr.* and *Eng.*
London, Utrecht [printed], 1868. 8⁰.

Agamemnon ; a tragedy, taken from Æschylus. [By Edward Fitzgerald.]
London, 1876. 4⁰.

The Agamemnon of Æschylus ; translated into English verse by E. D. A. Morshead.
London, 1877. 8⁰.
An instalment of the " House of Atreus," published in 1881.

The Agamemnon of Æschylus ; transcribed by Robert Browning.
London, 1877. 8⁰.

The Agamemnon of Æschylus ; with a metrical translation and notes critical and illustrative, by B. H. Kennedy. *Gr.* and *Eng.*
Cambridge, 1378. 8⁰.
A second edition was published at Cambridge in 1882.

Agamemnon ; translated from Æschylus by the Earl of Carnarvon.
London, 1879. 8⁰.

Scenes from the Agamemnon ; translated into English verse by Lewis Campbell, M.A. ; selected and arranged for the modern stage by F. Jenkin.
Edinburgh, 1880. 8⁰.
An instalment of a complete translation of Æschylus now in course of publication.

Æschylus' Eumenides ; the Greek text, with English notes critical and explanatory ; an English verse translation ; and an introduction, containing an analysis of the dissertations of C. O. Müller ; by Bernard Drake. *Gr.* and *Eng.*
Cambridge, 1853. 8⁰.

The Eumenides of Æschylus ; translated into English verse by the Rev. G. C. Swayne.
Edinburgh and London, 1855. 8⁰.

The Eumenides of Æschylus : a critical edition, with metrical English translation, by J. F. Davies.
Dublin, 1885. 8⁰.

The Eumenides of Æschylus, as arranged for performance at Cambridge ; the text in Greek and English ; the translation by A. W. Verrall ; the incidental music by C. V. Stanford. 2 parts.
Cambridge, 1885. 8⁰.

The Persians ; a popular version from the Greek of Æschylus, by John Staunton ; with photographs of Flaxman's designs.
Warwick, 1873. 4⁰.

The Persians of Æschylus ; translated into English verse by the Rev. William Gurney, M.A.
Cambridge, 1873. 8⁰.

Prometheus Bound ; a tragedy from the Greek, by T. Medwin.
Sienna, 1827. 8⁰.
Another edition was published at London in 1832.

Prometheus Bound ; translated from the Greek of Æschylus ; and miscellaneous poems by the translator, author of an " Essay on Mind " (Elizabeth B. Barrett, afterwards Mrs. Browning).
London, 1833. 12⁰.

The Prometheus of Æschylus and the Electra of Sophocles translated ; with notes intended to illustrate the typical character of the former ; also a few original poems ; by George Croker Fox.
London, 1835. 8⁰.
This translation of the Prometheus was reprinted with the author's " Death of Demosthenes " in 1839.

The Prometheus Chained ; translated into English verse by G. C. Swayne.
Oxford [Bristol], 1846. 8⁰.

Prometheus Chained ; translated into English verse by Charles Cavendish Clifford.
Oxford, 1852. 8⁰.

The Prometheus Bound of Æschylus ; literally translated into English verse by Augusta Webster ; edited by Thomas Webster, M.A.
London and Cambridge, 1866. 8⁰.

The Prometheus Bound of Æschylus ; translated in the original metres by C. B. Cayley, B.A.
London, 1867. 8⁰.

Prometheus Vinctus ; translated from the Greek of .Eschylus into English verse by Ernest Lang.
London, 1870. 8⁰.

Prometheus Bound (from the Greek of Æschylus), and original poems, by John Dunning Cooper. *London*, [1890] 8⁰.

The Septem Contra Thebas, the most popular of the extant tragedies of Æschylus, rendered into English verse by the Rev. William Gurney, M.A.
Cambridge, 1878. 8⁰.

The Suppliant Maidens of Æschylus ; translated into English verse by E. D. Anderson Morshead, M.A.
London, 1883. 8⁰.

SOPHOCLES.

The Tragedies of Sophocles, from the Greek ; by the Rev Thomas Francklin. 2 vols.
London, 1757-8. 4⁰.
Another edition appeared in 1766, with the addition of a dissertation on Greek tragedy by the translator. This was reprinted in 1809, but in 1832 the edition of 1759 was reprinted in 16⁰. In 1886 Professor Morley published Francklin's translation in the "Universal Library." Selections from Francklin's version were also included in vol. 50 of Sanford's Works of the British Poets, and in 1806 an acting edition of his Œdipus Tyrannus was printed at Reading on the occasion of the performance of the play at Reading School.

The Tragedies of Sophocles ; translated [by R. Potter].
London, 1788. 4⁰.
A new edition, with the author's name, was published in 1808. 8⁰.

The Tragedies of Sophocles ; translated into English verse by the Rev. Thomas Dale. 2 vols.
London, 1824. 8⁰.

The Tragedies of Sophocles; a new translation, with a biographical essay by E. H. Plumptre, M.A.   2 vols.
London, 1865.   8⁰.
A " second edition, revised," was published in 1867.

Sophocles.   The seven plays in English verse, by Lewis Campbell, LL.D.
London, 1883.   8⁰.
As shown below, six of the seven plays here collected had previously been published in three volumes between 1873 and 1876.

Sophocles; translated into English verse by Robert Whitelaw.
London, 1883.   8⁰.

The Dramas of Sophocles; rendered in English verse, dramatic and lyric, by Sir George Young.
Cambridge, 1888.   8⁰.

Three Plays of Sophocles—Antigone : Electra; Deianira, or the Death of Hercules; translated into English verse by Lewis Campbell.
Edinburgh, 1873.   8⁰.

The King Œdipus and Philoctetes of Sophocles; translated into English verse by Lewis Campbell.
Edinburgh, 1874.   8⁰.

The Downfall and Death of King Œdipus.   A drama in two parts.   Chiefly taken from the Œdipus Tyrannus and Coloneus of Sophocles.   [By Edward Fitzgerald.]
London, 1880.   4⁰.

Ajax of Sophocles; translated from the Greek, with notes.   [By L. Theobald.]
London, 1714.   12⁰.

Sophocles' Ajax.   The Death and Burial of Aias.   A tragedy; translated into English verse by Lewis Campbell.
Edinburgh and London, 1876.   8⁰.

An Imitative Version of Sophocles' Tragedy, Antigone; with its melodramatic dialogue and choruses, as written and adapted to the music of Dr. Felix Mendelssohn-Bartholdy, by W. Bartholomew.
London, 1845.   8⁰.
Another edition was published in the same year.

Σοφοκλέους 'Αντιγόνη. The Antigone of Sophocles in Greek and English; with an introduction and notes; by J. W. Donaldson.
London, 1848. 8⁰.

The Electra of Sophocles; presented to her highnesse the Lady Elizabeth; with an epilogue shewing the parallel in two points, the Return and the Restauration; by C. W. [Christopher Wase.] 2 parts.
The Hague, 1649. 8⁰.

Electra, a tragedy; translated from Sophocles, with notes, by Mr. Theobald.
London, 1714. 12⁰.

The Electra of Sophocles [translated by W. Drennan]; *Belfast*, 1817. 8⁰.

Sophocles. Electra; translated by G. C. Fox. *See* .ESCHY-LUS. The Prometheus of Æschylus, *&c.* 1835. 8⁰.

An abridged English version of Sophocles' Œdipus at Colonos; written and adapted by William Bartholomew to the music of F. Mendelssohn-Bartholdy.
London, 1848. 8⁰.

Œdipus, King of Thebes; a tragedy [in five acts]; translated from Sophocles, with notes, by Mr. Theobald.
London, 1715. 12⁰.

[A free translation of the Œdipus Tyrannus; by T. Maurice.]
London, 1779. 4⁰.
Part of the author's " Poems and Miscellaneous Pieces." The translation was again published in 1813 in a volume entitled " Westminster Abbey, and other poems," and again in 1822.

Œdipus, King of Thebes; translated by Sir Francis Hastings Doyle.
London, 1849. 16⁰.

Œdipus the King; translated from the Greek of Sophocles into English verse by E. D. A. Morshead.
London, 1885. 8⁰.

Œdipus the King. The dialogue metrically rendered by E. Conybeare . . . with the songs of the chorus as written for the music of Dr. Stanford by A. W. Verrall.
London, 1887. 8⁰.

The Œdipus Tyrannus of Sophocles, as performed at Cambridge, Nov. 22-26, 1887 : with a translation in prose by R. C. Jebb, and a translation of the songs of the chorus . . . by A. W. Verrall.
Cambridge, 1887. 8⁰.   —

The Œdipus Tyrannus of Sophocles ; rendered in English verse, dramatic and lyric, by Sir George Young.
Cambridge, 1887. 8⁰.
An instalment of the complete edition published in 1888.

EURIPIDES.

The Nineteen Tragedies and Fragments of Euripides ; translated by M. Wodhull. **4 vols.**
London, 1782. 8⁰.
A new edition in three volumes was published in 1809 ; the Hippolytus and Iphigeneia alone were published in Dublin in 1786. 12⁰.

The Tragedies of Euripides, translated [by R. Potter]. 2 vols.
J. Dodsley : London, 1781-83. 4⁰.
Editions in two volumes were published in 1808 and 1814, and one in three in 1832. The Alcestis and the Hecuba were published separately at Reading in 1809 and 1827, in connection with performances at Reading School. Selections from Potter's translation were also printed in Sanford's " Works of the British Poets."

Select Tragedies of Euripides ; translated from the original Greek [by J. Bannister].
London, 1780. 8⁰.
The Phœnissae, Iphigeneia in Aulis, Troades and Orestes.

Translations from Euripides ; by J. Cartwright, A.M.
London, [1868].   8⁰.
Medea, Iphigeneia in Aulis, Iphigeneia in Tauris.

The Medea, Alcestis, and Hippolytus of Euripides ; translated
into blank verse, with the choruses in lyric and other metres,
by the Rev. Henry Williams.
London, 1871.   8⁰.

The Bacchanals and other plays by Euripides : the Bacchanals
translated by Henry Hart Milman ; the other plays translated
by M. Wodhull, with an introduction by Henry Morley.
London, 1888.   8⁰.   *Part of Morley's Universal Library.*

The Alcestis ; translated into English verse, according to the
text of Monk, by the Rev. James Banks.
London, 1849.   8⁰.

The Alcestis of Euripides ; translated into English verse by
W. Fielding Nevins, B.A.
London, 1870.   8⁰.

Balaustion's Adventure ; including a transcript from Euripides
[*i.e.*, a translation of the Alcestis].   By Robert Browning.
London, 1871.   8⁰.

The Alcestis of Euripides ; translated from the Greek into
English, now for the first time in its original metres, with preface, explanatory notes, and stage directions, suggesting how it
might have been performed [by H. B. L.].
London, 1884.   8⁰.

The Bacchanals of Euripides ; translated into English by
Mons. Glouton.
Brighton, 1845.   8⁰.

The Bacchanals of Euripides ; translated by Henry Hart
Milman.
See ÆSCHYLUS.   Agamemnon, *&c.*   1865.   8⁰.

The Bacchæ of Euripides ; translated into English verse ; with
a preface by James E. Thorold Rogers.
Oxford, 1872.   8⁰.

The Cyclops : a satyric drama ; translated into English verse by P. B. Shelley.   Performed in the original Greek at Magdalen College School, Oxford, April 28 and 29, 1882.
Oxford, 1882.   8⁰.

Hecuba ; a tragedy [in five acts, and in verse, translated, with alterations, by Richard West].
London, 1726.   4⁰.

Hecuba ; translated from the Greek of Euripides ; with annotations, chiefly relating to antiquity [in five acts and in verse ; the dedication signed : T. M.—*i.e.*, T. Morrell].
London, 1749.   8⁰.
Another edition was published in the same year.

The Trojan Queen's Revenge.   [Hecuba, in English verse, by A. H. Beesley.]
London, 1875.   8⁰.

Aristophanes' Apology, including a transcript from Euripides [*i.e.*, from the Hercules Furens], &*c.* ; by Robert Browning.
London, 1875.   8⁰.

The Crowned Hippolytus of Euripides, together with a selection from the pastoral and lyric poets of Greece ; translated into English verse by Maurice Purcell Fitzgerald.
London, 1867.   8⁰.

The Crowned Hippolytus ; translated from Euripides, with new poems, by A. Mary F. Robinson.
London, 1881.   8⁰.

The Ion of Euripides, now first translated into English ; with preface and notes by H. B. L.
London, 1889.   8⁰.

Iphigeneia in Tauris ; a tragedy [in five acts ; translated by G. West].
London, 1749.   8⁰.
Part of an edition of the Odes of Pindar.

The Medea of Euripides ; translated by John R. Lee, M.A.
London, 1857.   8⁰.

The Medea of Euripides ; literally translated into English verse by Augusta Webster.
London, 1868.   8⁰.

Jocasta : a Tragedie [*i.e.*, the Phœnissæ] ; written in Greke by Euripides ; translated and digested into Acte by G. Gascoygne and F. Kinwelmershe.
Part of Gascoygne's Hundredth Sundrie Flowres bounde up in one small Poesie.
London [1572], [1575], *&c.*

ARISTOPHANES.

The Comedies of Aristophanes, translated into familiar blank verse, with notes, preliminary observations on each play, *&c.*, by C. A. Wheelwright.   To which is added a dissertation on the old Greek comedy, from the German of Wachsmuth. 2 vols.
Oxford, 1837.   8⁰.

The Comedies of Aristophanes ; translated by T. Mitchell. Vols. 1, 2.
London, 1820-22.   8⁰.
Contains only the Acharnians, Knights, Clouds, and Wasps.

The Comedies of Aristophanes ; translated into corresponding English metres by Benjamin Dann Walsh.   Vol. 1.
London, 1837.   8⁰.
Contains only the Acharnians, the Knights, and the Clouds.

Eight Comedies of Aristophanes ; translated into rhymed metres by Leonard Hampson Rudd.
London, 1867.   8⁰.
Reprinted, with the Greek, for the performance of the Acharnians, by Undergraduates of the University of Pennsylvania, in the Academy of Music, in Philadelphia, May 14 and 15, 1886.
Philadelphia, 1886.   4⁰.

Aristophanes. A metrical version of the Acharnians, the Knights, and the Birds ; in the last of which a vein of peculiar humour and character is for the first time detected and developed ; [by the Right Hon. John Hookham Frere]. 3 parts.
London, 1840. 4⁰.

Printed at Malta in 1839.

These three plays, together with Frere's version of the Frogs and a fragment of the Peace were reprinted in the collected editions of his works in 1872 and 1874. In 1886 Prof. Morley issued the three plays as a volume of his " Universal Library." In 1883 Frere's version of the Birds was separately reprinted at Cambridge [together with Mr. Swinburne's translation of the Parabasis], in connection with the performance at the Theatre Royal.

The Acharnians of Aristophanes ; translated into English verse by Charles James Billson, B.A.
London, 1882. 8⁰.

The Acharnians of Aristophanes ; translated into English verse by R. Y. Tyrrell.
Dublin, 1883. 8⁰.

The Birds of Aristophanes ; translated by the Rev. Henry Francis Cary. With notes.
London, 1824. 8⁰.

The Birds of Aristophanes, in one act. Being an humble attempt to adapt the said "Birds" to this climate, by giving them new names, new feathers, new songs, and new tales ; by J. R. Planché.
London, 1846. 12⁰.

The Birds of Aristophanes ; translated into English verse, with introduction, notes, and appendices, by B. H. Kennedy.
London, 1874. 8⁰.
See next entry.

The Birds of Aristophanes. The Greek text, as performed by members of the University at the Theatre Royal, Cambridge,

November, 1883; with the English version of B. H. Kennedy.
[With a preface by C. W.—*i.e.*, C. Waldstein.]
London, 1883. 8⁰.

The Ecclesiazusæ ; or, Female Parliament ; translated by the
Rev. Rowland Smith.
Oxford, 1833. 8⁰.

The Revolt of the Women ; a free translation of the Lysistrata
(acted at Athens, B.C. 411); by Benjamin Bickley Rogers.
London [1878]. 8⁰.

The Clouds of Aristophanes ; [translated by R. Cumberland].
[*London*], 1797. 8⁰.

'Αριστοφάνους Εἰρήνη. The Peace of Aristophanes, acted at
Athens at the Great Dionysia, B.C. 421. The Greek text revised ;
with a translation into corresponding metres and original notes ;
by Benjamin Bickley Rogers.
London, [1867]. 4⁰.

Πλουτοφθαλμία Πλουτογαμία : a pleasant comedie [in five
acts, in prose and verse], entituled, Hey for Honesty, Down
with Knavery ; translated out of Aristophanes his Plutus ; by
T. Randolph ; augmented by F. J.
London, 1651. 4⁰.

Reform ; a farce modernised from Aristophanes, and published
with annotations by S. Foote, Jn [*i.e.*, F. Wrangham. A
satire on Tom Paine.] *Gr.* and *Eng.*
London, 1792. 8⁰.
From the Plutus.

Plutus, or the God of Riches ; a comedy of Aristophanes ; by
Edmund F. J. Carrington, Esq., B.A., Oxon.
London, 1825. 8⁰.

The Plutus of Aristophanes ; translated into English verse by
C. P. Gerard.
London, 1847. 8⁰.

The Frogs ; a comedy ; translated from the Greek of Aristophanes, by C. Dunster, A.M.
Oxford, [1870 ?]. 4⁰.

The Frogs of Aristophanes ; translated by Charles Cavendish Clifford, B.C.L.
Oxford, 1848. 8⁰.

The Wasps ; the Greek text revised, with a translation into corresponding metres and original notes, by Benjamin Bickley Rogers, M.A.
London, 1875. 4⁰.